body of a girl

body of a girl

elisabeth barillé

Translated by Hubert Gibbs

HARMONY BOOKS / NEW YORK

Published by Harmony Books, a division of Crown Publishers, Inc., 201 East 50th Street, New York, New York 10022

Originally published in France as *Corps de Jeune Fille* by Elisabeth Barillé in 1986.
Copyright © by Editions Gallimard 1986.
This English translation originally published in Great Britain by Quartet Books Limited in 1989.

Harmony and colophon are trademarks of Crown Publishers, Inc.

Manufactured in the U.S.A.

Library of Congress Cataloging-in-Publication Data

Barillé, Elisabeth.
  [Corps de jeune fille. English]
  Body of a girl / by Elisabeth Barillé.
     p. cm.
  Translation of: Corps de jeune fille.
  I. Title.
PQ2662.A6877C613   1989
843'.914—dc20   89-24476
                                                CIP

ISBN 0-517-57552-3
10 9 8 7 6 5 4 3 2 1
First American Edition

body of a girl

Farouche, me? I love getting picked up. A man only has to satisfy two criteria: elegance of dress, lightness of wit. I appraise his appearance with my first glance; I make sure of his wit with the first drink.

'Why did you come up to me?'

By way of reply, the man passes a hand through his beard. In the Luxembourg this collar of fluff, undulating in the bracing air, lent him the grace of a pagan god; it had a completely white appearance. The spotlights cast a yellowish stain over it.

Immediately we arrived in this basement bar, the man buttoned up his check suit. When he had smiled at me near the large pond, the tails of his jacket were flapping like wings. He had appealed to me. I had responded to his smile; I had followed him.

We found room for ourselves in two of the leather easy chairs arranged in pairs around low tables. He greeted a guy sitting near a piano. Though the latter was beardless, he bore a strange resemblance to him: the same light eyes, suntanned face, the same slimness which was accentuated by the neat cut of the suit. He raised his hand, then immersed himself once again in a magazine.

1

A shrill laugh made me start: a young woman with a bare forehead, bronzed as well, was bending the nape of her neck over her neighbour's shoulder; she had upset his glass. The drink and slices of fruit had spilled over the carpet.

I'm not used to smart places, above all if in them I detect an air of complicity on people's faces, a secret understanding between their bodies, as in this room the walls of which are covered in beige suedette. An affluence shared intimidates me. The waiters in waisted jackets have the look of heirs about them. I feel gauche, vulgar almost, in my flounced skirt the colour of which – fuchsia – sticks out like a wrong note. What was so seductive about me that he made his approach? I ask him again, on the look-out for a compliment like a puppy awaiting its sugar.

He watches me.

'I came up to you because of your neck. Do you know it's fascinating? I was following you from the puppet theatre. It was all I had eyes for, its fragility and pallor. At a certain point you turned round. The colour of your eyes surprised me. I pictured them being light; they're black. Ingres would've chosen you as a model.'

Pose for Ingres with my round cheeks, my abrupt movements!

I burst out laughing.

He looks crabby: 'Are you in the habit?'

'Of being picked up?'

'I haven't picked you up.'

A few faces look up. The barman stops flourishing his shaker and throws me a fierce stare. I have laughed too loudly. I have infringed the rules of this bar. How would I know them? I have only been living in Paris a few months.

'If you haven't picked me up, why have you brought me here? Your interest in me is surprising. There's nothing exceptional about me.'

2

He leans back in the armchair, his mouth half-open. He has the yellowed teeth of a heavy smoker.

'That's why I adore girls! They have no idea of their real beauty. They look at their bodies in the same way as a Philistine does a Dutch still life. Just as virtuosity captivates simpletons, so their most obvious charms blind them. You're proud of your nice breasts. Am I wrong? No. Compared to the line of your neck, your breasts are quite ordinary. Remember that.'

Nestling in its half-bra, the said bust quivers with indignation. I did not come here to be insulted! If I had been on the terrace of a café, I would have seized my shoulder bag and 'See you, bye-bye!' But elegant surroundings smother my instincts.

'Thanks for telling me about it.'

Realizing he has hurt me in view of the face I am pulling, he quickly adds: ' . . . On the other hand I do like your outfit. Patent-leather pumps, pink socks, matching tee shirt and skirt; and those pearls round your neck, in your ears! Do you work in fashion?'

'No, I'm a student. A modern-languages student.'

'A student,' he mutters.

He seems disappointed. I do not match up to the standing of his lordship. I am neither a model nor a stylist. Just a literature student. Out of inclination.

The barman rouses us from our silence.

'Ah, Robert! The best barman in Paris! The man of a thousand and one cocktails! A remsem cooler as usual.'

'With a glass of hot water?' Robert specifies.

Gratitude glimmers in the blue eyes.

'Yes. I still have a painful throat. Not too hot, the water, just warm. What about you?'

'I can't stand cocktails. Do you have any tea?'

Robert eyes me with disdain.

'We do not serve hot drinks.'

'I only drink tea. China tea. Preferably lapsang souchong.'

'The Fever isn't a tea room, *mademoiselle*,' Robert counters in an even voice.

My neighbour taps me on the hand.

'Stop playing the spoilt child . . . just choose a cocktail. I've told you, these are the best in the capital.'

'OK, a remsem.'

Robert withdraws, his torso even stiffer. The man gives a sigh of relief. He must be known here: he calls the barman by his Christian name.

'You're going to be won over: one measure of whisky, one measure of ginger ale and the peel of an entire lemon. A *must*!'

Couldn't he express himself more simply? I wouldn't have followed him in the Luxembourg if he had spoken like this. I dislike pretentious people.

I begin to fiddle with my collar of imitation pearls, suddenly hating this gimcrack jewellery, the straightforward trashiness of which had amused me. Jewellery for kids.

'You seem disappointed that I'm studying literature. What's wrong with university?'

He gestures vaguely. On the forefinger of his right hand, two coiled serpents wind themselves around a heart.

'University is meant for mediocrities who can't make up their minds. Don't argue. You know perfectly well that you're wasting your time there. Learn a trade or go round the world, but for heaven's sake don't stay at university, above all if what you're doing is literature!'

'But I love literature.'

You would have thought you were hearing a defendant in the dock.

He bursts out laughing: 'Yet another reason for leaving in a hurry! I wonder why you haven't done so sooner if literature fascinates you as much as you claim it does. Do you take any sort of interest in your teachers labouring the same old points?'

4

'That's going too far!'

'Not at all! I too went to university.'

'Pooh, thirty years ago at least!'

'No, *mademoiselle*, twenty-five years ago. But in a quarter of a century the teachers haven't changed: sour-faced intellectuals who all like to think they're writers. Writers!'

'Some do write. My comparative literature professor has just . . . '

'They write! What do you know about writing, do you mind telling me?'

I see him again in the Luxembourg, motionless beneath the drizzle. How did I imagine that he could flare up so quickly?

From the inside pocket of his jacket he draws a lacquer case, out of which he takes a cigarillo. Robert, who has not taken his eyes off us, dashes towards him, a lighter in his hand. He mutters his thanks; greedily inhales the smoke, then, having expelled it far in front of him, proclaims: 'I am a writer.'

A writer! The golden halo encircling him suddenly strikes me as of a substance more rare than the smoke, similar to the gaseous emanation which streams out of Aladdin's lamp at the moment when the genie appears. A writer, in flesh and blood! Sitting next to me! Not just a professor who writes. But a writer, a real one!

My amazement could invite laughter.

I spent my adolescence in a village in Anjou. There, little reading was done. The bookshop-cum-stationer's in the post office used to offer a few paperback classics for the schoolchildren, and best-sellers. Works which were outside these two categories were available only on order. They used to arrive every Saturday. Among the novels it was rare for one of them not to have been set aside for me. I would read it like the letter of an exiled relative, nurturing the hope that I would fathom the daily life of the author between the lines. It intrigued me, I who wished to write. The characters interested me less than the novelist; I was often hungry for more. At the time of official holidays, the manager of the bookshop used to invite a writer to a signing session. I would never go. As the bookseller was content to meet his clientele's tastes, his guest was not conspicuous for his literary merit. Even had he been an 'author', I would not have gone along. What was the use of announcing that I admired his work, when I wanted him to talk about himself to me? But what writer would have anything to do with personal secrets in a bookshop-cum-stationer's? So I would leave them in that vague Olympia which I called 'the world of letters' with an irony tinged with envy.

My look of astonishment amuses him. He smiles as he pushes the glass towards me, the rim of which is frosted with sugar.

'Just taste this drink to recover from the shock. To think you've never met a writer . . . !'

He leans towards me.

'Now that you're in on the secret, I will admit the real reason for our encounter.'

I throw him an uneasy glance. He slowly brings the cocktail to his lips, takes a mouthful, puts the glass down on its paper mat. How he plays with my curiosity! He looks at me again, then, clinking the cubes of ice, he raises his glass towards me.

'You're a character out of a novel. My future novel. I already have the plot in my head. The central character was missing. When I noticed you in your pink socks, braving the rain like a little soldier, I knew that you were this character.'

He seizes me feverishly by the hand.

'What's your name?'

'Elisa.'

'I won't have to alter the Christian name. It's perfect. Elisa, I've been working on this project for several weeks: a girl disclosing the secrets of her life . . . her life . . . ' he continues earnestly.

He observes me out of the corner of his eye. I don't flinch.

' . . . of her sexual experiences. I'm not shocking you, am I?'

'Not in the least. It's a great subject!'

My cocky self-assurance has been put on; a sudden quivering has taken hold of me. Alcohol goes to the head. That sort of intoxication sharpens the mind.

The writer moves up to the edge of the easy chair and beckons to me to come closer.

'Elisa, for me you are that girl. Don't ask me why, I've no idea. A question of feeling.'

'So you want me to tell you everything . . . '

The excitement mounts all the time. Unless this is an idea which has germinated without my knowing it, an idea I have nurtured since childhood, an idea not truly so but one of those ambitions you formulate in an undertone: 'My destiny is to be a heroine!' Some of the kid's desires you don't forget.

'Rest assured, I won't insist that you bare yourself completely. You can tell me what you feel like. You need only recount a few affairs, memories: your first kiss . . . I intend to follow my heroine up to the age of twenty.'

I quote him those books the glossy covers of which depicted a child with brown plaits, a girl in Tyrolean costume, then a mother surrounded by her children, finally a grandmother with a slightly insipid face in an unchanging setting of mountain pastures: *Heidi Grows Up, Heidi the Girl, Heidi and Her Children, Heidi the Grandmother, In the Land of Heidi*. I remember every book. My childhood is so close to me.

'Heidi! My younger sister used to own the entire collection. How old are you to have shared what she read?'

'Twenty-two.'

'That's amazing!'

'You thought I was more.'

'Less! Much less! I have before me the woman-infant type. The woman who augurs as many delights as dangers!'

I shrug my shoulders. Do writers always express themselves so extravagantly? Is this one making fun of me? I casually reply that I grew up without realizing it.

'I got older without noticing it as well.'

He awaits a word of protest.

The man he had greeted rises to his feet and leaves the bar without glancing at him. A shadow passes across the writer's features. His lips flutter imperceptibly as though he were talking to himself. The artificial light really does not flatter him. He appeared younger in the Luxembourg as he walked into the wind with the jauntiness of a schoolboy. He starts to fumble around in his jacket.

'Are you looking for something?'

'My notebook . . . Ah, there it is,' he says, flourishing a green spiral pad which he opens at the first page. 'I'm all ears.'

'What do I have to tell you?'

'What I've just explained to you. Do you agree to be my heroine, yes or no?'

'I'd like to a lot but I have nothing fascinating to reveal.'

'Listen, I hate wasting my time.'

He closes his notebook and nervously taps on the table with it. He is too well brought up to leave but the idea of it has no doubt crossed his mind. I would miss an opportunity – perhaps the only one – of realizing one, even two dreams: to know a writer, to recognize myself in a book.

'Well then, don't you remember anything about your childhood?'

Childhood. The word has too soft a resonance to evoke the disorder of my early years: bric-a-brac building up a house in *tuffeau* stone in front of a vegetable garden, a table laid for Russian Passover, forget-menots stuck on to the frozen top of the *kulitch*, a navy-blue dress with a bib collar, the topaz an uncle used to wear on his little finger . . . Insignificant details. A diminutive: 'sweetie', pronounced with a strong Russian accent by my grandfather. Some nicknames: 'Fatso', 'Froglet'. Scenes juxtaposed without logic like the successive shots of a film's credits. Minor incidents – falling into a frozen pond; charming habits – the tooth placed under the pillow for the fairies. A single illness: viral pneumonia, not even tuberculosis. Neither drama, nor separation. A colourful childhood certainly but too quiet to arouse the interest of a writer.

'Why aren't you saying anything? I'm not asking the impossible, just a scene. I'm not sure I'll incorporate it into the novel. Perhaps I'll only keep the odd detail, smell . . . Listen . . . '

He breaks off to take out a second cigarillo from the case lying on the table. Robert dashes up with a lighter, then immediately moves off. The writer takes a drag, screws up his eyelids: 'The most exact of my memories remains the odour of my mother's blouse. When she returned from milking the cows, she would hang it in the corner of the cowshed, in the spot where the churns were put. Her blouse smelt of fresh milk, sweat and sea spray. We lived on the Normandy coast. The farm now belongs to my sister. I go back there occasionally. Taking advantage of being alone for a moment, I slip into the cowshed: I look around for the blouse . . .'

His confidence leaves me puzzled: a little peasant, this elegant writer, this intellectual . . . I glance at his pale hands with their narrow wrists. What if he were lying? Do novelists always tell the truth? When one fantasizes the whole day long, doesn't one begin to confuse imagination with memory? Does the pleasure one takes in conjuring up the past spring from the sensation of reliving it or from the opportunity given to embellish it? What if I too were lying? What if I were inventing a perfect storybook childhood? I laugh softly. Hurt that I have not been more affected by what he has said, he asks me sourly: 'Have I said anything funny?'

'Nothing at all.'

I sit facing him, my elbows planted on each side of the empty glass.

My childhood also reminds me of a smell. That of books. They were not made of words but of mingled scents. Face powder, old fur, worn leather, *Bourjois* soap, dust and that indefinable perfume which sticks to clothes worn intimately by relatives who have died a long time ago. I would read in a wardrobe. An oak wardrobe, as wide as the wall. I spent hours in it, permitting myself as little air and light as possible. It contained a hundred or so children's books and comics, hat boxes, a super-8 film projector, four or five panamas each fitting one on top of the other, a mahogany casket crammed with singed lace and reels of cotton, the wardrobe of a grandfather, of two grandmothers, of a mother who kept her wedding dress there and a ten-year-old child curled up like an Inca mummy on the throne which the pile of books formed. I would spend entire days, my bottom perched on the albums of *Mr Castor*, my nose stuffed into marmot jackets. Generations were hanging above me. High-spirited ancestors passed through my reading. The fairies would wear crêpe dresses; the explorers tapered breeches; the animals wore veiled hats, felt hats. My stories reeked of family reminiscence. Despite everything, I liked suffocating among these old clothes, I enjoyed it. Sometimes I would bury my head in them, conceal my mouth, my eyes. Everything would fuse then: the body of a girl – my mother – the body of a grandfather, whose double-breasted suits and handkerchiefs scented with Chanel Number 5 evoked a strangely effeminate image for me, and my body.

I fall silent for a moment to check that he has not

lost interest. He motions that I carry on.

'You were talking to me about sweat . . . the wardrobe used to smell of sweat, cold tobacco and . . . and . . . desire. I must admit that in this wardrobe . . . do you understand what I'm trying to say?'

He listens to me, his look intent, his chin resting on his palms. He listens to me as I have never before been listened to. I thought I was surprising him but suddenly I am the one feeling caught. I stand up so brusquely that the two glasses wobble. He just manages to catch them.

'I have to leave you.'

I rummage in my bag to hide my confusion. He seizes my hand.

'This is on me.'

Without looking at the bill, he leaves a hundred francs on the table, stands up as he tightens his silk neckerchief and buttons his jacket.

His silence disconcerts me. I was expecting him to ask me to justify my leaving. Normally . . . But how can I compare him with other men? What can I conclude from his sophistication or his sensitivity? How can I interpret this reserve which I find so attractive? I might have thought he was cold, had I not seen him flare up, calm down, flare up again, then become still like the ocean in the dead season. He was born on the Normandy coast. He has the open expression of a son of the Vikings, their slim physique. I find him . . . seductive is not the word . . . attractive despite his age, because of it perhaps. I like polished men.

'We'll see each other again.'

His tone brooks no refusal. I lightly finger the beads of my necklace.

'What's the point . . .?'

Why do my lips twist out these meaningless words? Why can't I stop myself from playing the flirt?

'Am I of so little interest to you? Do I strike you as too old, too serious?'

11

Why does his sincerity not arouse my own?

'You must be joking. I'm the one who is too childish, too superficial for you. You'll quickly get bored with me.'

When he smiles, his beard bristles like an animal.

'I'll take the risk. Tomorrow at four o'clock, in the jardin Marco Polo. You know, opposite the avenue de l'Observatoire, not far from here. On the left-hand bench as one is coming from the fontaine des Quatre-Continents,' he specifies, before blowing me a kiss from his fingertips, while he watches me leave.

I have returned to the boulevard Saint-Germain. Headlamps, gleaming coachwork, neon lighting and shop windows coloured by the summer collections, prolong the flurry of the day in a final scene which jars and confuses. Confused is what I am myself. Excited, anxious, charmed, apprehensive. My emotions squeeze up and stick together in my body which seems too narrow to contain them all. I feel I am besieged like the pavement, which is trampled over by the passers-by whom I jostle with my elbows. I run. I stumble. I laugh. A writer! I have met a writer. I have spoken to a writer. He wants to see me again, to get to know me so he can slip me into his novel. He told me so. I have therefore conquered him . . .

I notice the distorted reflection of a streaking, pink silhouette in the shop windows: my body, unstable, fleeting. A pink form without face.

I dash to the edge of the pavement so as to run unimpeded. I have never felt such lightness. I run open-mouthed to let the overflow of exhilaration gush out. Freed. From what? It does not matter. I am aware only of the firmness of my muscles, the heat of my cheeks, the sparkle in my eyes which occasionally meets with the lewd wink of a motorist advancing slowly along the congested boulevard. I would agree to go with anybody. That guy with brown curls in his Golf GTI. For ten minutes now he has beckoned me towards him every time his car, held up by the traffic jam, comes to a halt abreast of me. I laugh. My cheeks are burning. My body feels even lighter.

When he cries out: *'Bellissima mia!'* at the junction of the rue Saint-Jacques, I hear the writer murmuring like an echo: 'You are my heroine.' The Golf spins round to park in front of the fast-food joint where I have positioned myself, hand on hip. The door opens. I slide on to the black leatherette seat. The guy hardly looks at me. He moves off, the tyres of his car screeching, and turns into the rue Saint-Jacques.

'My name's Marco; what's yours?'

Lightly he strokes my unconcealed thigh. At his hand's contact I cross my legs. He gives a slight cough, then leans towards the cassette radio.

'Michael Jackson. OK with you?'

I nod. He turns the volume up full blast. I'm perspiring, overcome by a sudden urge to get out. The car isn't moving. Marco drums the leather-encased steering wheel with his fingers. His flaccid profile, his permed hair make him look like an emperor from a Roman cameo. Seated as far away from the steering wheel as he is, his arms are stretched out as though he were holding the reins of a chariot. His rayon shirt does not properly hide a heavy body.

'What nightclub do you want to go to? *The Privilège, Bus Palladium, Bains-Douches, Tango,* what's your scene?' he says, casting a quick look over my cheap skirt.

I've had enough. I push the door open forcefully and throw myself out.

'Come back, baby!'

I disappear down a one-way street. A Renault 5 is emerging at the same moment. I just step back in time, as I answer the blare of his horn with a shrieking laugh. I start to run again, passing from the roadway to the pavement, my heart beating loudly. An impudent kid. Patent-leather pumps and pink socks.

I slam the door of the studio, take off my shoes, pearls, tee shirt and stretch myself out, panting. My emotions are exciting me. Blushing at the bar. My heart pounding when the man told me that he was a writer. My thigh trembling just now in the car.

Abruptly they return with the same intensity. They swell, rumble and gush down towards my pubes. If I don't plunge a finger into my crack, if I don't stick the forefinger of my left hand up my ass while my right hand titillates my clitoris, if I don't jerk myself off, I'll explode.

To come more quickly, I shout out abuse.

'You bitch! Tart! Little whore!'

The whore who was acting coy at the bar, by pulling down her pink skirt; the whore who in the Golf didn't have the guts to be a real one, she was sweating so much from fear, but who had let herself be pawed in the conviction that she was 'living her life to the full'.

What dreams I had for my life before coming to Paris! I would spend hours in my room; the window looked out on to a wine producers' co-operative. I would try out different hairdos, make-up. I read women's magazines which recommended me to avoid pearl-coloured make-up when one had brown eyes. I subscribed to *Elle*. I used to give my mother knitting patterns and recipes. I cut out certain beauty treatments, took the inspiration for my clothes from what models were wearing. I wanted to appear Parisian.

15

In Paris, I was obsessively afraid of seeming provincial. Above all with men. A girl from Anjou struck me as less desirable than one from Paris. There I was thin; here, almost plump. There I only had to wear a very tight skirt to be pointed at; here I would go unnoticed. I increased the number of affairs I had, less out of the thirst for conquest than to reassure myself. How many men? No matter. Enough not to doubt myself any longer, too few to despise myself completely, like Countess Livia, the heroine of *Senso*, these words of whom I had copied down into my diary: 'My spirit soars by humiliating itself.' I thought I understood the meaning of this phrase.

It is my body I am humiliating when I masturbate. It is my body I am damaging. It is my body I am punishing in this way for having grown up, for being no longer the one Mummy nicknamed 'her little Tanagra'. Her life is over, the one who used to wear two brown pigtails and a gold cross at the end of a chain, whose mother would come to tuck her up in bed. Did you know Mummy, that I masturbated almost every night? A piece of blanket in my mouth smothered my grunts. The fear of being surprised by you greatly increased my pleasure. I would hear you climbing the stairs. The door would half-open; I closed my eyes. You would lean over me, lightly touch my forehead. I would pretend to be asleep. I have always pretended: to be a nice child, a good pupil, a Parisian, a liberated girl.

My melancholy prevents me from coming. I sit up, slip on my panties which I had torn off to caress myself more deeply. I shiver. Why keep turning over my childhood? I have the feeling of succumbing to a peculiarity of the elderly.

Our family meals used to last for hours. Through the dining-room window I would see the light grow dim; the main street become swollen with shadows. I was no longer hungry; yet I held out my plate to my mother. I thanked her for her generous helpings. I emptied my plate in silence. My body weighed down on me. I felt disgust that I was stuffing myself in this way. I felt worthless. I felt a coward: out of gluttony I was betraying the exceptional woman I wanted to become: the explorer, the actress, the dancer, the novelist. How could I be their equal when I was filling my stomach with rich and succulent food? Only one expedient to win back their respect was left to me.

I would ask for permission to get up from the table. It was given to me at the cheese course. I would go up to my room. I shut the door, drew the curtains. I lay down on the crocheted bedspread; I jerked myself off. This was my revolution. Masturbating struck me as more provocative than smoking or going out with boys.

My orgasm was slow in coming. Mummy interrupted me by calling out: 'What are you doing up there? I'm bringing in the pudding. Come down!' I obeyed. I tidied up my hair. As I left my room, I sniffed my fingers. On them was the scent of my revolt.

When I sat down among them again, Grandfather took me by the shoulder: 'Plunged in your books again, my dear . . .?' I named him a title at random. Then I held out my plate for the rum baba, submitting to the last act of the family ritual in a rush of subservience no less than of greed.

What a wonderful recollection for my writer! Would I go as far as to admit to him that I play with myself? I almost told him so at the bar but I abandoned the idea at the last moment. I was afraid of his reaction. I would have scared him. For him my sex life must boil down to a boyfriend, to problems with the pill. I noticed his sardonic look when he asked me 'to recount a few affairs'. Would he understand why I abuse myself, why I masturbate with the intention of hurting myself? Is he really interested in me, in my childhood? He actually has only one desire: to fuck me.

I get dressed unhurriedly.

Perhaps I am being unfair. He did not act in an uncalled-for way towards me, he hardly even stroked the nape of my neck. How he drank in my words when I was relating the episode in the wardrobe. How attentive he seemed! Then he left me gracefully, as an Italian would.

I open a formica cupboard full of packets of pasta. Shells? Mini-lasagne? Linguine? Bows? Tagliatelli? Just spaghetti? Pasta, gastronomy for the single girl. I eat it every day, varying the sauces – garlic, Roquefort, tomato, gruyère.

I have been living alone for a year.

I announced my departure one summer evening. Daddy was finishing Bach's first cello suite. He was playing it in front of the window which opened on to the garden, a well-kept little garden with trays of geraniums; and a pile of manure at the end of the vegetable patch.

'It's decided. I'm going to study in Paris. I'll take a room. I'll find a part-time job.'

I wanted to escape the monotony of the provinces.

Mummy had rushed out of the kitchen with a crumpled look, as if I had betrayed a secret between her and me. My father again played the first suite with more intensity. This was no farewell he was addressing to me but his thanks, he who had never been able to study. He always spoke of it. This was his wound.

I forgot the oil to prevent the pasta from sticking. Mummy couldn't stop giving practical advice about how to prepare a cheese soufflé, look after polished furniture, iron delicate fabrics, about the art of using up leftovers. She knew it by heart. The earnestness with which she lavished it upon me endowed it with a gravity which prohibited me from disregarding it.

Mummy was pursuing a goal through her advice: that of binding me to her as she had herself been bound to her mother. She sensed her defeat. This was possibly the reason for her melancholy. She knew that I would elude her, that never would I be a model wife, a mother. She harboured a discreet animosity because of this, which she concealed less and less as she grew older. My father remained a stranger to this painful complicity. He lived in his regrets and his dreams. He would have liked to be a mathematics teacher or a conductor. In the daytime he used to sell caravans; in the evening he played Bach on an old cello.

The pasta is overcooked. I chuck it into the dustbin. The writer must be having dinner in a fine restaurant with an elegant lady, the type who crunches appetizers with fastidious little bites, appreciates white, rosé and red wine, savours yet indulges her appetite, talks about everything naturally. A real Parisian, in fact!

I sprawl on the divan, a cushion against my stomach. What a delightful evening! If my writer saw me like this, he would change his heroine straight away!

Do something! Just take out the typewriter and compose as moving a childhood memory for him as possible. You will give it to him tomorrow.

I imagine myself cavorting about in the place de l'Observatoire. I walk down the middle of the avenue shaded by chestnut trees. On each bench clusters of young mothers, wearing loden and moccasins, are reading or knitting, one eye on their little boys. I pass in front of them striding firmly, my head held high. 'I am free. I have an assignation with a writer. My life is far more adventurous than yours.'

Tomorrow I will get dressed up. I will put on a straight lamb's-wool skirt with a shiny finish. I will clip on some earrings, round ones which attract the light. I will be holding a reinforced envelope. If he asks me what it contains, I will reply: 'You'll find out when you get home.' I do not want him to read this childhood memory in my presence. He will discover it at home like a love letter which you open at the day's end, having fingered it, turned it over and over, breathed it in since the morning.

'This guy makes me feel romantic,' I murmur as I take out a sheet of paper.

I have been trying to write something for an hour now without success. Normally writing comes easily to me. At exam time I hand in my script before the others. I dash off an essay in an afternoon. I shower my friends with chatty letters. They answer me with carefully chosen postcards; occasionally they do not reply. The electric typewriter has encouraged my inclination, just as a motorbike can make an adolescent who has only ridden a moped, delirious with speed. Hardly have I switched it on, reviving its discreet humming, than the words come to me effortlessly. I write with an intoxicating fluency.

I'm losing my temper. I bite my nails in impatience. 'A childhood scene. A short scene of twenty lines . . . ' I pull out a Camel, chew on it without lighting it. Why am I incapable of stringing two words together?

Pride. Fear of disappointing the writer. Fear that he will consider my story of no consequence.

My recollections lack sparkle. I might compare them with the sea snails which I used to collect during the holidays on the beach in the Roussillon. Each one the same, grey, tiny. When I had filled up a bucket, I would throw them back into the sea.

I'm losing hope. I run a finger over the edge of the machine in a gesture of surrender. I will be happy with a trite conversation on the bench of a square. Will he even want to see me again? I doubt it. He will go in search of another heroine with a richer store of memories and that's all there is to it.

Why shouldn't I describe my masturbation sessions to him? For fear of shocking him? Agreed, he is of another generation. But after all, he is a novelist. To write is to free from prejudice. To write is to go beyond taboos . . . What could I be offended at? Catching my father screwing my mother? Yes, that's it: hearing Mummy come beneath Daddy. The scene. God knows, it has haunted me.

Now my fingers are striking the keys.

I am playing the explorer at the far end of the garden. Mummy appears on the steps in an apron: 'It's dinner time!' Regretfully I fold the sheet which I had pitched as a Sioux tent and return towards the house, lingering on the way.

I hated eating with the family. When hunger overcame me in the middle of the afternoon, I would go upstairs to the kitchen. Without making a sound, I would hurriedly swallow several spoonfuls of *gratin* which Mummy had left in the oven. Sometimes she caught me. She would remain in the doorway, hands on hips, draw her little figure up straight and exclaim sarcastically: 'So, we're eating like a Jew, are we!' (Where she had learnt this expression, I still do not know.) I fled into the garden, my lips moist, shattered at having been called a Jew. Not, on the contrary, that I felt any shame. When I thought about it again in the toolshed where I had taken refuge to recover my composure, this tartness, which was contemptuous coming from my mother, made me quite proud. Jewish I was because different. Solitary and lucid like a Jew in exile.

I would experience this feeling of strangeness at dinner time sitting opposite my father, between my mother and grandmother. Grandfather 'presided' at the other end of the table.

They opened their mouths at the same time.

I would listen to them chewing, swallowing while the presenter on the telly spoke in a clear, calm, voice.

21

I watched them grabbing the bread with brusque movements, sucking the chicken bones. Grandfather's lips were always gleaming. He would furtively wipe away the scraps of meat stuck to the corners of his mouth with his tongue. My father fed himself in haste. He smacked his lips as he drank his soup and only spoke once his plate was empty. Grandmother was unable to eat without sauce or the juice of fruit running down her chin.

My mother was the most discreet. Her education. As a girl, she had learnt deportment. She hardly opened her mouth, handled her fork with delicacy; placed it with the prongs on the edge of the plate. Under the table, her thighs were slightly parted. My mother perspired. She had spent an hour the day before preparing this chicken in aspic. Admirable, my mother! What a glittering role! Once again I observed my father, silent, concentrating hard.

While they ate I thought only of 'it', of their doing 'it' after the evening film. Their bodies sated, their desires unwound by the habit. I would say to myself that in two hours' time they were going to be doing 'it', in the same way as they ate. In silence, smells and mucous membranes mingling, in the shadowy light of that room which I entered as I would a crypt, a deserted synagogue.

A nice twist!

The second Camel I light is delicious. Such a story will hook my writer! He will demand the rest. What happened after dinner in the double bed beneath a crucifix and two lithographs. So I will have to make it up; I never caught them. Except for one evening in the kitchen . . .

I entered abruptly; I always entered abruptly. In front of the sink two silhouettes were fused together, leaning against the draining board of Italian porcelain.

Twisted my mother, as though dislocated. A body

22

which would collapse were two arms not clasping it. Barely clothed this body, in a dressing gown partly open. The knees were slightly bent, as though ready to kneel. Facing her a dark mass, crammed into a leather overcoat. My father. His thick neck disappeared in the wide lapels. He had put on his new ankle boots. He held my mother by the shoulders like a rag doll. He embraced her. He hugged her. He smothered her. He clenched the dog's lead in his hand. The lead brushed my mother's bare feet.

They caught sight of me. My father released his grip. I stammered out an excuse then ran off, slamming the door.

Sigh. Smile. Suspicion. Rag. Dog. Bitch. Lead. Bottom.

Words, ideas were coming to me which I drove away like a bad dream, my throat dry.

From the window of my bedroom I saw my father walking the dog. He would go round the block as he normally did. My mother was washing the dishes. I could hear the clinking of glasses in the sink and the voice of Yves Montand which she was listening to as a distraction.

As poky as an antechamber, the place Henri-Honnorat separates the jardin du Luxembourg from the avenue de l'Observatoire.

I arrive there at a quarter to four, my heart thumping.

I pronounce 'place Henri-Honnorat' in an emotional, almost worried tone, just like an exile who repeats the name of the station, stamps it on his mind as he disembarks in his town of welcome. You might think of a lover at his first assignation: on the way which leads to the desired one, he notes the names of the streets, shops, the colours of the cars, even the dress of passers-by, so as to fix a moment in time which he wishes to remain unforgettable.

Fourteen minutes to four. I have pushed open the small entrance gate of the place Marco Polo, chosen the left-hand avenue because its chestnut trees with their denser foliage make it darker. My forehead, my cheeks are on fire. By the tips of my fingers, as if it were burning them, I am holding the book into which I have slipped the reinforced envelope. Spinoza's *Ethics*. The philosophical essay should temper the audacity of my appearance: a see-through blouse over a leather skirt.

Five to four. A ball rolls towards me, pursued by a little boy in flannel shorts. I prepare to kick it back to him but on the sudden reflection that too wholehearted a release of my thigh might risk ripping my skirt, I check my movement and stand aside both sheepish and furious with myself. In vain do I deride girls who doll themselves up for their men; I'm like them. Worse: I'm doing it for a guy I hardly know.

Four o'clock. I approach the fontaine des Quatre-Continents. He is not there. I sit down, get up again immediately: he would conclude that having arrived first, I have waited for him.

The fountain has been drained. Two little girls with bare legs are stumping around the basin laughing. Their agile bodies, the savagery of their playing despite their laughter, the brutality of the blonde who is knocking the little redhead about with a large branch, the latter's docility: everything about them takes me back to the memory of a scene in the holidays.

I was twelve years old. My pal would not be long. She lived in a remote farmhouse a few kilometres away. I was looking out for her red bicycle. There she was. As usual she came through the courtyard. We played every day together during the holidays. Her name was Arlette. She was said to be 'well developed for her age'. She had rather sturdy calves and broad shoulders. Her smock pressed tightly against her bust. After our tea – buttered bread sprinkled with cocoa – we ran into the garden towards the toolshed.

The door did not open easily; ivy had grown in the hinges. Arlette forced it with her elbow.

We groped our way in the darkness to the walnut kneading trough. Arlette took out a candle. She stuck it into the neck of a bottle which she placed on the ground. I struck a match.

She tied me up to the trough. This was the first rule of the game. She pulled so hard on the rope that my arms were burning. I was careful not to protest. I was forbidden by the second rule to utter a word. I was required by the third to take deep breaths from some cotton wool soaked in Gifrer's ether. A lapis-lazuli bottle. A fragrance sweet as honey which you would breathe in through your nostrils, more disturbing than Mummy's scent, Vol de Nuit. Arlette pressed the cotton wool over my face. I began to suffocate. I signalled that she should go. This was the fourth rule of the game: Arlette had to leave me alone, shut in for an hour.

Arlette returned too soon. I told her to leave me; she refused. We quarrelled. She mounted her bicycle and disappeared. I stayed on the trough without moving, my hands unbound, my eyes wide open.

I didn't feel anything, I didn't blackout. I became irritated. So I tried to frighten myself. I told myself that I was going to die, that my body would rot. 'You are going to die, you fat pig!' I kept saying.

I knew no other swearword.

Ten past four: still nobody. The little girls are playing.

Ten years later, in a train at Bologna station. Pierre was holding me beneath him by my wrists. He was hurting me. I smiled. He lowered the curtain. I wriggled under him. He bit my breast. I burst out laughing. 'Bitch,' he shouted, as he made to slap me. I raised myself up on my elbows, licked my lips without taking my eyes off him.

'Say that again.'

Pierre stared at me intently, scared by his insult. How had he been able to call her this? She, his love, his almost sister, his darling, his pet. Bitch.

But as I continued to smile, Pierre stifled his apology. Perhaps she really was a bitch.

Twenty past four. I wait, my flat shoes placed on the bench, oscillating between fury and resignation. My pride calls upon me to depart: I cannot be patient for more than a quarter of an hour.

There he is. Great strides bring him hurrying along.

'Forgive me. Phonecalls I didn't think would ever stop. My editor, a colleague, one or two women and two journalists. Have you been waiting long?'

'No, I've just arrived.'

Seeing the shoes which I did not have the presence of mind to put on again, I begin to turn red. He does not notice. He is quite breathless.

'I ran . . .'

He collapses on the bench. He looks like a leading man past his prime with this aviator's jacket. He retains only a silk scarf from his elegance of the day before.

He catches his breath. His cheekbones regain their pink colouring. Striated with tiny blood vessels, they alone reveal his Norman origins. He looks at me closely with laughing eyes.

'I find you again as I left you. To be honest I was afraid of this second meeting . . .'

' . . . Wondering whether you hadn't embellished the portrait?'

'No. The model is a great deal more charming, more seductive even than yesterday.'

I do not share his thoughts. The stiffness of his gestures, the furtive glances which he ventures ceaselessly, arouse a feeling of uneasiness in me. I hold out the envelope. He snatches it from my hands. I hasten to add that this is not a declaration of love.

'What is it then?'

Suddenly realizing, he bursts into laughter.

'I bet that it's a childhood memory! You wrote it on beautiful white paper. I am no teacher. I didn't demand a dissertation, an essay, one of those idiotic things which are taught in the classroom under the high-flown heading of "French Composition"! "What was the best moment of your holidays? Your first disappointment? When did you experience the feeling of injustice for the first time? What is the moral to be drawn?" What stupidity! Very fortunately for me I was hopeless. Which only goes to prove the meaningless-ness of the term a "literary vocation"!'

Why this curt tone? His sudden loss of temper the day before when he criticized university had already struck me. He lost his composure, tapped his thigh with his hand while his left eye, which is smaller than his right, began to blink slightly, as it is doing at this moment.

' . . . At what age did Sterne start writing? And Whitman? Even Proust. *Les Plaisirs et les Jours*, small beer compared with . . . '

He stops short as soon as he realizes that I am observing him, dumbfounded. His left eye stops moving.

'Where was I . . . Ah yes, the envelope.'

He weighs it up and spits out: 'You want to compete with me?'

Although his mocking tone a second earlier has prepared me for it, the belligerence of this riposte revolts me.

'Hey, your status as a writer doesn't give you the right to be disagreeable! I'll leave if you go on!'

He scratches his beard. He folds the envelope, puts it away in the inside pocket of his jacket and proposes that we walk.

We stand up. We take a few steps. He pats my cheek with that grudging affection of parents when they are scolding a small child.

'Keep writing. It's a healthy occupation. But don't think that this whim exempts you from confiding in me orally. You have committed yourself to it, my dear. The heroine's fate is on your lips, which are too pretty for you not to use.'

His compliments ring hollow. The relaxed way he dresses is affected; his conversation is even more so. So much pretence ought to put me off; it pushes me towards him.

The chestnuts are swaying in the wind, heralding rain.

'What a fool to bring you here. We're going to get soaked. Let's go and find a shelter.'

I protest for fear that he may drag me to the Fever. Yesterday as I was leaving the bar, I noticed a black plaque on the door engraved with golden lettering.

THE FEVER
Private Club

'I don't wish to be shut up indoors.'

'You're shivering. Do you want my jacket?'

'It's awful.'

'Is it the weather which is making you so nervous? Come on, no discussion. Take this jacket and follow me. I know a place which will calm you down. I bet you have never been into the Val-de-Grace.'

'What's that?'

'You're doing an Arts course, you claim to be interested in literature – therefore in history – and you don't know about that masterpiece of classical French art! The Val-de-Grace is an architectural grouping built on the orders of Anne of Austria under the direction of Mansart and Lemercier. Although it was converted into a military hospital, the main body of the buildings has lost nothing of its grandeur. As for the church . . . a gem . . . Here, take a step backwards. Don't you see that perfect dome, it looks like a breast . . . Are you Catholic?'

In a hesitant voice I reply: 'I've been baptized. I've made my first communion and I've been confirmed. I used to go regularly to catechism class. A little later I frequented the chaplaincy of the lycée. I've kept my faith.'

I am lying. My faith deserted me as does our childhood. A day comes when we notice that toys leave us

29

indifferent, that shop windows at Christmas no longer fill us with wonder, that cakes make us put on weight, that our parents will die. Likewise one day we realize that there is no point whatsoever in praying and that the saints up above do not hear us. I used to read about their lives in strip cartoons in those weeklies for the young which Mummy would give me after mass. Charles de Foucauld – the colour of sepia – smiling at his murderers. Bernadette Soubirous as a child, a blue shawl over her shoulders. Saint Francis of Assisi, my favourite. So young. So pure. I had chosen a scene in which he stretches out his arms towards a flock of birds to illustrate the 'announcement' of my first communion. Mummy had retorted that this was not 'a girl saint', that it would be better to pick Saint Anne or Saint Geneviève as my godmother. Faced with my insistence she had given in, declaring to my father who remained unmoved by faith, revelation and other mysteries (his admiration for Bach being 'instinctive' according to him): 'Your daughter is an eccentric.' I would have preferred her to call me a mystic. A mystic I had become ever since the famous discovery . . .

'Do you know anything about Saint Blandine?'

'Of course! A martyr from Lyons who was thrown to the lions with Saint Pothin around 170 A.D. . . . '

'That's not the most important thing. Take out your notebook. I have something to reveal.'

The writer complies, all excited. In his agitation he knocks into a slightly-built old man who is hobbling along the middle of the avenue. He mutters an apology. Then he leans against a chestnut tree.

'As a child I liked being alone. I would spend entire afternoons in the attic. I would reread old letters to unknown addressees. I unfolded petticoats. Fragile and showy, these old clothes turned me into a page or a princess. I enjoyed myself without making a sound. Rummaging around in a box of books, I noticed a missal with a silver clasp. Its ivory binding had gone completely yellow. When I opened it, a piece of paper fell out. I picked it up. It was a card with jagged edges, with a heart painted in its centre encircled by a crown of thorns and roses. On the back, a little blonde wearing a V-necked dress offered her slender body to two ruffianly soldiers, armed to the teeth. Why was she smiling when one of them was levelling his pike at her, the point trained on her breast? "Could suffering cause pleasure? Voluntary suffering?" The discovery disconcerted me. I had sat down on the edge of the box, pondering. Blandine threw me into confusion with her hand on her breast, the other on her loins, with her eyes raised heavenwards, her look beatific, silly, amorous. She had plump, pale pink cheeks – that hawthorn pink of coloured lithos. A little virgin. A little tart who was trying to be the centre of attention by throwing her hair back like a real star, as though she were saying: "Look how desirable I am!" Suffering, pleasure, death, desire: that was what the crown, the heart and the roses concealed.

'I suddenly wanted to suffer myself. This was a violent, instinctive desire, more profound than the one which spurred me to feign a blackout in the toolshed. This was no longer a game. Blandine's right hand was laid on her breast, I placed mine on the same spot; her left hand beneath her navel, I put my left hand lower down. Do you understand?'

The writer nods. He passes a hand over his beard as though he were searching to add something.

'To sum up, you discovered orgasm through Catholicism. Obvious, obvious, my dear! Bernini, the illustrious Bernini . . .'

The shower interrupts him. I dash beneath a chestnut; he does not move, his face exposed to the rain. I hear him declaiming: ' "We are carefree when we are seventeen and have green lime trees on our walks!" Arthur! My poet, brother, master!'

What a madman! I shout out that he should rejoin

me, that he will catch cold if he carries on. That makes him laugh. His oration grows in intensity. A roll of thunder forces him to return to me.

'I wouldn't tire of reciting *Les Illuminations* whatever the time, the place – perched on my father's tractor, my body in the straw, on the way back from the harvest; bending under the pail of scraps which I was going to take to the sty to feed the pigs.'

'You used to read Rimbaud on the farm?'

'The country isn't full of people who don't read, you know, Miss Student.'

End of discussion. No point in explaining that I have known enough farmers (those who came to the house to sign up for insurance policies; Mummy ran a small farm insurance office to give herself something to do) to conclude that rarely do they read Rimbaud.

The shower is coming down even harder. The leaves bow beneath the heavy drops. My mascara must be running. I will look like those mourners in ancient tragedies with rings of charcoal round their eyes. The rain is more becoming to the writer. It has returned the lively sparkle to his look which had attracted me in the Luxembourg. Does he perhaps remember the freshness of the sudden Normandy downpours? Does he perhaps still feel the child's exhilaration at being soaked to the skin, like a captain at his helm riding out the storm?

'Would I have had the strength to leave the family farm without Rimbaud? My parents' life of toil weighed on me, although I was keenly aware of its dignity. I saw them working without any goal other than to continue working. I saw them achieving what their parents had achieved with worry and privation their only rewards. They lived modestly. They did not dream. They acquiesced. And I, I was their son. And I read Rimbaud. And I cried out to the cows: "Reality is too complex for my lofty nature." Who else could I

32

have confided in?'

Here he goes, beginning to affect me again! Who is he anyway? A poser or an idealist? A socialite or a loner? Are we so different, he and I?

'If only you realized how I would like to get to know you better . . . ' I say timidly.

His face clouds over.

'They all say that at the beginning.'

'Who are "they"?'

'Women. My admirers.'

'Who says that I admire you! Just who do you think you are? You don't impress me at all!'

He makes a movement towards me; I dodge him. He catches hold of me. We would be perfect for the reconciliation scene twenty minutes before the end of the film. Forgetting sarcastic remarks and hesitations, the heroine sinks into the hero's arms. Outside shots: high winds, driving rain or raging sea.

'Forgive me. I've hurt you. You're different from other women. My problem is that I generalize. Don't hold it against me . . . Let's go back to our tree.'

He takes me off by my waist towards our shelter. 'Swift, the author of Gulliver's Travels, said roughly this: "I detest the human race but I like Peter, Paul and James." Women disappoint me. But when I meet one of them and get to know her, I renounce all my misogyny.'

He wipes away a drop of water which is trickling down my cheek. We smile at each other.

'For me there are two types of women. The musical ones and the others. By "musical", I don't mean musicians – not all musicians are musical – I mean those whose presence fills their surroundings, whose bodies slip every hold; those whose every movement creates harmony; those who you hope for a moment carry the answer with them . . . If you like Schumann, you would understand me. My sister was musical. We used to write our homework next to each other in the

33

living room. As I contemplated her with eyelids so lowered over her exercise book that she seemed asleep, I would feel touched by grace. Her slim neck, her curls frothing over her pale forehead, the curve formed by her shoulder, elbow and hand placed flat on her pencil case; each detail of her body enraptured me. I was both elated and at peace. "Nothing can happen to me as long as she is by my side!" I would murmur to myself, while a slight anxiety crept over me as if I were picturing the surly farmer's wife my sister was to become. Whenever I listen to Schumann's *Fantasy in C major*, I think of her. You too, Elisa, you're musical.'

'No, my father is. He adores Bach, above all the *Suites for . . .*'

'You weren't listening to me! You weren't listening to me when I was telling you first of a profound reflection about the nature of women, second of a feeling which is dear to me. If I don't interest you, what are you doing here?'

I could retort that first he wanted to see me and not the other way round; second . . . what's the point?

'You're wrong. I was listening to you. What you said so moved me that my senses faltered and my hearing was . . . '

A writer cannot resist a well-turned phrase. He clasps me to him and expounds his theory about 'musical women' a second time.

The rain has stopped. A ray of sunlight tears open the clouds. We waltz down the boulevard du Port-Royal. Five steps away from me, his hands in his pockets, he whistles a tune, teases a little girl who is waiting for her mother in front of a baker's shop. This is quite the way it should be. I'm humming. The sky has the luminous quality of a Poussin painting. The expression is my father's. Why think of him when everything is lighter than air? Why evoke him still

34

vigorously playing Bach?

I was working hard at my Greek in the dining room which led through an archway to the sitting room where he normally practised. I heard the first notes of the saraband from the fifth suite. He was attacking it too slowly for my liking. I immersed myself in Homer again. He came to a sudden halt, stood up, moved towards me, cast an eye over my book, smiled at me and said: 'That's true happiness: playing Bach in the company of one's daughter. Being carried away by the one and feeling proud of the other. No pleasure can be as intense.'

Then he went off as discreetly as he came, took up his bow again and pressed it over the strings, as though he wanted to bring from them a flow of tears which I knew were now forming in his eyes. His sentimentality irritated me. Out of cynicism I was going to masturbate in the loo. But as long as the phrasing of the cello was unfolding, my body, the brave little soldier standing to attention, dared not tremble. I listened to those musical repetitions . . . Soon, unable to take it any longer, I ran to my room. Everything was swaying there. The smell of fanny rose. The saraband went on.

Somebody bind his hands, cut mine off! Block up my ears! Restrain me! Ruin me! Corrupt me! Exhaust my craving for orgasm, assert myself before my father, before Bach! The frauds. They kept their game well hidden. Bach, head of a numerous family. My father . . . They too got hard-ons. The phoneys.

After reaching the church of the Val-de-Grace, bitter disappointment. The gates are closed.

'What bad luck. I so wanted you to see the dome painted by Mignard; Pierre, naturally.'

'Next time . . . '

'All the same, in the middle of the afternoon.'

He pushes the entrance gate with his elbow, looks for a bell, swears, returns to the gate, puts his head between the bars.

'Is anybody there?'

How strange it is: the figure which his proud bearing would suggest he has, is diminished when seen from the rear. His hips don't appear wholly symmetrical. As for his head . . . he makes me think of certain busts by Rodin. Innocuous when you contemplate them from the front. Worrying, when, by walking round them, you discover a roughly hewn block where everything merges: the hair, the nape of the neck, the joins of the shoulder-blades, the shoulders. To detail this shapeless mass, images of still-born children come to me, images of swollen faces, burst lips, gashed cheeks . . . I must be tired.

He returns towards me, a smile on his lips.

'There is one hope. A man in the courtyard indicated that I should enter through the hospital. What's the matter? You're all pale . . . '

'I've got to go home.'

'Do you feel unwell?'

'No . . . Yes . . . I want to leave.'

'That's silly, I could have shown you the dome. Do stay.' He strokes my chin. 'I still haven't been treated to one of your romantic adventures.'

A dribble of saliva spurted from his lips when he uttered the word 'romantic'. I'm only thinking one thing: get the hell out.

'I'm going.'

'Very well,' he says, as he shapes to bow.

His farewell makes me tremble. Does he want to leave me for good?

'Wait! How are we going to see each other again?'

'Give me your phone number.'

He tears a piece of paper out of his notebook. I scribble down my name and number on it. He stares at me for a moment then moves off whistling.

Why did I leave him like that? Because he struck me as less attractive from behind? Because the flesh which lay in folds on his neck made me think of soft fabric? Does a writer's body matter more to me than his soul? Would I have turned Sartre down because of his physique? No, I would have let him kiss me; if not more. Despite his age, the writer is a handsome man. He conjures up Drieu la Rochelle for me. A bearded Drieu. A litheness in the leg, a misty light in the eye. Unpredictable. Caustic and tender. Considerate and offhand. Elusive. So many men give themselves away so quickly. So many men dwell on personal confidences during the first date. So much talk for a simple night out.

The rue Saint-Jacques seems to go on for ever. It's raining again, small cold drops. What if I went to Hélène's? She lives at number eighty. She will offer me mint tea and macaroons; I will put up with her cats and her chatter. I will nibble in silence. I am not going to talk to her about the writer. She will insist on details as she wriggles about on the sofa in such a supple way that you expect to see her leap up again. What would I tell her? That he is a writer? I know absolutely nothing about him. I don't even know what he has written. I have never asked him, too happy to talk about myself, to stop being the girl who listens without passing judgement, the girl who offers consolation.

I walk past number eighty.

My girlfriends are self-pitying; I myself take care not to be. Whingeing is not aesthetic! Mummy used to snivel over a badly cooked leg of lamb. I couldn't bear to look at her red eyes. Obscene. I occasionally cry. So I plant myself in front of a mirror to make sure that I do not look like my mother.

Melancholic by nature, I suppress my spleen out of pride. My girlfriends say I am invulnerable.

I move forwards crabwise. I try in vain to straighten my trajectory, I zigzag to the pavement. Walking blues.

I go into a bistro, decorated in the old fashion. Only one table is free; I sit down at it, while ordering a double espresso.

The one brought to me is covered in a thin layer of froth just the way I like it. The coffee restores me. Scalding the throat, tasting strong, I drink it in one gulp. It will warm me for one or two hours. It nourishes me.

I savour my solitude.

True, I don't have a friend but 'friends'. The distinction is an important one. Exclusive friendship holds no appeal for me. I do not value loyalty.

Ten or so girls criss-cross Paris to relate their misfortunes. They unroll their bundle of heartaches, dazing me with anxious questions, with names. I try to pay attention. I nod to make them believe that I am listening to them. I am elsewhere. I observe them. Their bodies do the talking.

We were watching television. A literary programme about James Joyce, I think. He loves that sort of novel. Stream of consciousness. That's right isn't it? Beforehand? We did not touch each other or if we did, we would apologize at the slightest contact, quite embarrassed. He was far away. You know what I mean.

We were coming back from Dinar. We had had a good dinner: sole in champagne sauce. The road was empty. We looked at it in silence. Before the meal? He had given me one of those looks. I don't know how to tell you. Sly and deep. Understand?

I know, I understand you, my dears, squatting crosslegged. My gaze, my hearing snaps you up, as you sit confidingly on your chairs and fidget, like on the day of an exam.

Then for no reason he suddenly runs a hand through my hair. Like that, very slowly, without taking his eyes off the screen. I don't say a word. I'm frightened. I don't know why.

All of a sudden he takes hold of my hand, without looking at me. His left hand stays on the steering wheel. What's got into you? We were now talking more formally to each other; that was good.

They become animated as the story progresses. They stretch out their legs, tuck them up again; they pull down their skirts; toss back a rebellious lock of hair; one or two bite their lips as they recall the moment when they understood that 'they were going to do it'. They are becoming excited. They are all aquiver.

He continues to caress me from the roots of my hair to my throat. I'm trembling. Molly is Joyce's most heartbreaking character. Without taking his eyes off the screen, he fondles my shoulder, my breast.

He's insistent and takes my hand again. I have forgotten everything: the looks, the sign language, the little display of affection just a short while ago. I put my hand in his. He kisses the palm very tactfully.

They copy the man's gestures exactly. They remember the smallest details. A small computer has recorded them in their heads.

I take advantage of the credits to dash to the kitchen. I light a Gauloise. What have I landed myself in now?

I draw our two entwined hands towards me. I kiss them. I've lost the first round.

39

Afterwards? In bed? What words? What phrases? Didn't they say anything? Did they remain silent?

They no longer remember. Only the first gesture counts, the seismic jolt which shook their bodies. Barely five seconds. The distance is closed. The claim is staked. Beforehand, they could neither fart, nor perspire, nor overeat in this man's company. They swallowed discreetly. They touched up their make-up in the loo.

Conceal what is going on underneath. Cave, membrane, mucous membranes.

The man makes the move. The man's hand through the hair; the hand which seizes, squeezes the shoulder, thigh, foot. The hand which feels.

Test the ground. Prepare his entry into a body which has already surrendered.

I motion to the waiter.

'Excuse me, do you sell cigarettes?'

'No. Across the road.'

'Thanks.'

'Any time. Goodbye, *madame*. Thanks a lot.' I used to feel proud when, as a child, I dispensed these expressions. Today this politeness irritates me.

In spite of my independent air, I remain a good little girl who wants to please everybody. In Paris, I discovered the politeness of the English, all in disguises and silences; a skillful balance of courtesy, hypocrisy and ingenuousness. When men want me, I give in to them without a fuss. Turning them down would hurt them. Turning them down would make them even more talkative. I don't need persuading to go to bed. Simpering manners, mock modesty, shows of virtue strike me as more indecent than parting one's thighs, a smile on one's lips. Men only see passion in this. They interpret my good manners as loose morals or warmth of feeling.

Would the writer understand this concern to reveal

nothing of oneself?

Since meeting him, this attitude has weighed on me. In his presence I feel the need to open my heart. Is it his promise to make a heroine of me? My life sublimated like Joan of Arc's, Louise Brooks's! My life embellished, turned into a novel . . .

Three days have gone by since our last meeting. He has not rung me.

For three days now I have no longer gone to the university. A few worried friends have phoned me. I have replied grouchily that I had better things to do. One of them reminded me of the exam we were supposed to revise together; I hung up on him abruptly. To hell with studying! The way the writer derided it has diminished the limited appeal which I attached to it. I will not take my class exams at the risk of disappointing my parents who are following my academic progress from their small town, as they have watched over my development. I have always been a good student; they felt not a little proud of my successes, although they would have preferred me 'to do' political science or business school. They think of literature as a pastime. They read in the train or on the beach: my father political best-sellers, my mother romantic novels. They write out of duty: letters to tradesmen, insurance contracts, New Year's cards.

I feel I am shallow. I spent the morning asleep. I dreamt of the writer. He seemed angry. He was saying to me, 'Do you always behave like this with men?'

The ringing of the telephone makes me start. What if it were him? By the singsong tone of her voice, I recognize Hélène.

'I've got an hour to kill, can I come round?'

The untidiness of the studio and my washed-out

complexion will arouse her suspicions. A sharp girl, she will pester me until I confess. I will confess nothing. Let her come. Her chatter will amuse me. What are friends for if not to take one's mind off oneself?

'Don't be long.'

'Just give me enough time to buy some strudels and I'll be right with you!'

Hélène is brilliant, greedy, generous. She is Jewish. We met at university, didn't see each other when she started as a journalist on a militant review, then met up again by chance.

There are motives for every friendship. For ours, Hélène's Jewish origins are one of them. To have her as a friend is almost to be Jewish. I feel Jewish. Is it to counter my mother's anti-Semitism? Is it because of my matt colouring, my dark eyebrows which are out of place in a family of blonds? Some reasons are too deep for me to understand.

This could simply be coquetry; it is an innermost expression of myself, which is almost physiological. I feel Jewish as one feels ill.

Hélène sometimes asks me to accompany her to the Rachi centre where she takes part in conferences. On those evenings I overdo the kohl and blusher to accentuate my looks, to appear the least 'goy' possible. My fear of being unmasked makes me feverish.

My throat is in knots. Hélène responds to smiles. I keep my eyes riveted to the programme. I do not want to meet anybody's glances; I would see my imposture in them.

Hélène is three quarters of an hour late. She comes in looking upset. The box of cakes is being shaken about against her bust.

'I'm sorry, a stop-press wire . . . '

'Now that you're the assistant chief editor, I can no longer slam the door in your face.'

I bring her in by the elbow. She walks with the dainty steps of a Japanese girl, my beautiful oriental journalist! Charms of gold stir in the shadow of her throat. She lets herself fall heavily into a chair as she hitches up her skirt.

'I've had enough of this job!'

'Patience. In five years' time, you'll become chief editor.'

'Chief editor of what, do you mind telling me? Of a rag without a future? Zionism, I've done that. As for the community . . . '

She stares at her shoes; another new pair with netting in silver leather.

How could she have noticed my pallid face; hers is even more colourless! What do I do? If I manage to combat my friends' melancholy, Hélène's leaves me helpless. She makes the most of everything she has: disagreements at the paper, the war in Lebanon, her sister's divorce, the poor weather, a dog dead in the road. Depression clings to her soul.

I head for the kitchen to make her the strong tea she likes. She follows me. I sense that she is going to talk, leaning against the sink, while I fill the electric kettle with water, scatter some Darjeeling in the teapot, cut up a lemon into thin slices. The kitchen incites women to confidences.

My mother, normally miserly with her indiscretions, gave in when she spent the afternoon at the farms of her sisters-in-law. They lived between Varenne and Longué, on the northern bank of the Loire, 'the wrong side', the side where you find neither country houses nor caves in the rock, but prefabricated villas and plastic greenhouses. A beaten track led to the five farms which were a few kilometres apart from each other. My aunts were called Paulette, Bernadette, Eliette, Ginette; Rolanda was my favourite. She used to give me grains of maize for me to make necklaces.

I remember their legs dried out by the sun, their bare feet on the green lino, the nylon blouses which they would put on next to the skin, their brown armpits; their hair, which in women of this area grows low on the forehead, was brown as well. My aunts and my mother used to natter in the kitchen beneath the paper streamer for killing flies. They shelled white beans for preserves. Seated in a corner, I leafed through mail-order catalogues; my aunts did not buy any magazines. Occasionally one of them would lower her voice. The others brought up their chairs. I pricked up my ears. 'Is he unhappy at his age?' or else, 'When you've got a man, you see to it that you keep him.' I didn't understand a thing. At four o'clock they made themselves bread spread with *rillettes* and drank red wine diluted with water. My mother asked for some Vérigoud. She poured a glass of it for me, then sent me into the courtyard to play. I ran off to the rabbit hutches.

The kettle is singing. I place the strudels on a plate. Hélène passes a finger over their coating of sugar.

'I can't stand remaining single.'

In the time it takes for her to utter this phrase, Hélène has changed. Her body has sagged. It appears petrified. Her lips have grown pale. It's a shapeless mass, a Mater Dolorosa crudely hewn in stone. She twists her mouth. The sob does not come. Her despair is too theatrical for me to believe it. Evasively I suggest that she should go out a bit.

'Go out: that's a joke! I'm suffocating in this community. I'm going round in circles!. . . If I weren't Jewish, I would be anti-Semitic! You can't understand what it's like to be Jewish, what it is not to allow oneself to look at boys who aren't. You have never experienced our family law which commands you "to get married, my daughter, and give us some beautiful children". Where is the freedom to love?'

When Hélène puts her glasses back on, it's a sign

that she is going to cry. I draw her towards me, ruffle her curls, kiss her on the cheek.

'You're always dramatizing everything! Your situation bears no similarity to that of your grandmother who was forced to be married, or of your mother who never had the right to go out before she got engaged. Your father doesn't keep an eye on your comings and goings.'

'Why should he? I don't go out. I'm on my own, on my own!'

'And what about me? Aren't I as well?'

'You are out of choice; I am because I'm compelled to be.'

'What are you on about? Come and taste these strudels instead of talking nonsense!'

She refuses the plate which I offer her. Greedyguts Hélène! She who crosses the whole of Paris to buy goodies at Goldenberg's!

Her disarray affects me but I allow none of it to show. Love-sickness is catching.

'Stop being so serious, Hélène. Stop racking your brains when you don't have to. Allow yourself the pleasure of being irresponsible from time to time.'

'You're making fun of me. You don't care what I feel. I really sensed that you didn't want me to come on the telephone. What have I done to you? You don't like me any more? Is that it? You don't like me any more, you too? Answer me! Answer me or I'm leaving!'

I did not know how to reply; Hélène has left. After the door closed, I thought I heard a sob. I did not call her back. I gulped down the strudels. The flaky pastry stuck to the roof of my mouth. I drank a cup of tea then took out a packet of biscuits. I munched them in pairs. I began to feel nauseous. I opened a pot of strawberry jam.

I am eating to punish myself. I have hurt my friend solely to enjoy seeing her grow ugly through misery. This is something to make me feel ashamed about; I'm not. I throw myself on to my bed, stuffed, disgusted. My body feels heavy. By tomorrow I will have put on a kilo. I am a real pig. I begin to masturbate. I have reached the stage where self-loathing is becoming exciting.

I slip in the cassette of Act II of *Don Giovanni*. Mozart helps me come. The vocal entrechats of the Countess, Elvira, or Donna Anna hasten my orgasms.

The recitative begins. What does it matter if I do not grasp the meaning of the words. Donna Anna's voice is all that counts.

Donna, you give me gooseflesh. Donna Bella. Belladonna. Your cries of sensual pleasure, of love's anguish spark and crackle. Your voice is in colours: red, violet, pink. The colours of my flesh. Into which I stick my fingers. Your voice accompanies my hand. It rises and falls, describes curves, traces circles, ebbs and flows. I'm going to come. Wait for me, Donna!

Donna continues her song.

> *Calma, calma il tuo tormento*
> *Se di duol non vuoi ch'io mora*

She holds her breath, thrusts it to the back of her throat to give her voice more vibrato, to prolong her voice until the note breaks, to delay the moment when pleasure topples over.

> *Se di duol non vuoi ch'io mora*
> *Forse un giorno il cielo ancora*
> *Sentira pieta di me.*

Her voice climbs ever upwards. My pleasure mounts; higher, higher throughout my body.

The music bursts apart.

I stop the tape. I stand up. With my legs like jelly I lean against the bookshelves. It's wonderful to come. Then I think the opposite. Coming is frightening. I can see it in the mirror. My face is red, puffy. I who wanted it to be as smooth as a mask of volcanic glass, as pale as the marble of steles and memorials! I examine my narrowed eyes, my tense forehead, my creased cheeks, my lips glistening with saliva. I try to understand. I stick my tongue out. I screw my eyes up. I squash my nose against the mirror. I draw back. I have my father's low forehead, my mother's round chin; so much for the legacy. I come up close enough again to make out the light down which darkens my upper lip and the tops of my cheekbones. Beneath the down, my skin. And beneath my skin? Might I find my true face there? Where is it? Is it the one which the mirror sends back to me, flayed by pleasure? Is that the face, barely indistinguishable from my flesh, which was mine at birth and which appears only at the moment of orgasm?

I'm on my way to the Fever. I decided to go on impulse. I went out with the sensation that I was moving forward along a diving board, several metres high. Either my leap succeeds, or I will break my back. Again I either arrive looking radiant, my nipples hardened by the cold, my breasts thrust out in front of me, my back arched with the effort, the very young sprinter reaching the finishing line. Heads turn towards me. The writer stretches out his arms. Robert hails my coming with a novel cocktail, the Return of the Prodigal Child: one measure of champagne, a half-measure of apricot juice, a suspicion of brandy, a drop of raspberry liqueur . . . Or I will be kicked out.

'So we made ourselves look pretty to pick someone up, did we!' a man calls out from his car window. I shrug my shoulders and carry on walking between the cobblestones. At the corner of an alleyway my courage wavers. It collapses when in the window of a fashion boutique, the lights of which are still on, I become aware of the incongruity of my dress, embroidered with plastic sequins. I look like a Barbie doll. The writer may well shudder at it. It is by the elegance of his companion that the man of taste is recognized.

How am I going to justify my unexpected arrival? By admitting that I can't stop thinking of him? He will think I am in love. When a man declares he loves me, I leave him. The writer will do the same. The affair will be over! Back to university, my class exams, teacher-

49

training. Pierre. We will talk about getting married . . .

'Elisa! What are you doing here?'

I have reached the Fever without realizing it. The writer was leaving at the same moment.

'I . . . I was going . . . to the cinema.'

'In that sequinned dress you would be the star.'

He inspects me from head to toe, a sardonic smile on his lips. More than ever his face calls to mind that of a capricious and sensuous god.

'Your wonderful Moroccan broach hardly goes with your dress but it works. Seeing you in all this finery prompts me to ask you out to dinner.'

'I can't . . . The programme is about to start and . . .'

'You're lying as surely as you breathe, my darling. You're not going to be a crybaby. It's charming and terribly feminine to lie. Give me a smile. There. Tell me now, where were you going dressed like that?'

'To the Fever; to see you. You hadn't been in touch with me for three days. I didn't understand why.'

'My novel! My novel, darling! I am in the full flow of creativity! Thanks to you!'

The door of the Fever opens. We step aside to let a small bald man, wearing a black polo-neck, go past. The writer's eyes follow him in amusement. With a wink he announces that this is a colleague. He slips his arm through mine. We take the best-lit side of the road. My dress sparkles. He finds it wonderful. He finds me delicious. He says that I inspire him; that his instinct had not let him down in the Luxembourg, that the heroine of his novel would be more moving than Anna Karenina, more piquante than Albertine. Laughing I protest. I feel good, hanging on his arm. I want to sing like Gene Kelly as I twirl around the streetlamps. I want to eat croissants on the embankment, climb to the Sacré-Coeur, run away with him to the seaside. The picturesque aspect of this alley in the *sixième arrondissement* completes the illusion: I'm making a film.

The writer is skipping rather than walking. I have never seen him so playful.

'When inspiration is slow in coming, you find that it's madness to write, but when it sweeps you away . . . you feel like a titan. To write a novel is to make a crossing by yourself; the mind weathers every storm. Assailed by doubt, discouragement, it must hold fast. It is when resisting that it triumphs. Writing is a combat. Do my remarks seem excessive to you?'

'You don't have the ravaged face of the warrior after the battle. You're looking rather well to me.'

'You're joking! Look at me in the light. Can you see these rings? Do you notice my pallid skin? I have lost weight,' he adds, passing his hand between his stomach and his belt. 'You don't seem convinced.'

'Not really . . . In fact I wonder what you are writing.'

'You already know: the inner life of a girl,' he says tersely.

'But tell me what . . . Talk to me about your earlier novels.'

'I'm not interested in them.'

'But that's absurd . . . '

'Absurd! You're the one who is absurd, Elisa. I thought I understood that we had agreed on this point. It is not because you are recounting your life to me that I am bound to share mine with you. You're not a novelist as far as I know.'

'But friendship . . . '

He looks at me pensively.

'Friendship . . . Do you imagine that such bonds can be created after three encounters? I know; you women, you become friends very quickly. But when I see what perfidious things "best friends" do to each other, I shudder! I hope that you're not one of those. Let me finish. We may become friends one day; at which point I will open up to you. For the time being, let's stay as we are.'

51

'Under these conditions, I can't. Ring me when you experience the desire to see me. But if it's just to purge yourself of your artist's moods, don't call.'

'You haven't understood what I meant.'

'I have understood quite clearly.'

'I was greatly looking forward to having dinner with you . . . Do you like seafood?'

'What will we discuss if you refuse to talk about yourself? Me? I'm tired of that. We will enjoy our oysters as we lap up the iodized water in satisfaction, just like hundreds of silent couples.'

I am not being truthful, I would like to accompany him. Dinner with a writer: that would be the first time. I could make a wish . . . To spend two hours alone together. To encourage him into confiding in me. To seduce him a little. Just a little . . . To find out.

'Do you think that two people have to chatter endlessly when they are together? Won't you be able to put up with my presence, as I will appreciate yours? I will observe your hands when you pick up your fork, your mouth when you slip an oyster into it, your nostrils when you raise a flute of champagne to them, your eyes when the waiter brings a flambéed soufflé – like all women you doubtless can't resist desserts – I will also look at your . . . '

'There's no point in going on.'

He heads for the edge of the pavement and begins to look out for cruising taxis. That he can go so rapidly from great excitement to indifference is just a little wounding. It is not without attraction as well. I don't know what to feel. I don't know what to do.

He hails a Mercedes which pulls in a few metres further on. He gazes at me without saying a word, grabs hold of my wrist and makes to kiss my hand. I withdraw it.

My grandfather's friends, invited to five o'clock tea, would greet Mummy in this way, as they had been taught to do in Russia in the days when they were still in charge. Before holding out her hand, Mummy would wipe it furtively on her apron which she had not had the time to untie. They bowed towards her; she would turn red then withdraw her hand very quickly. One might have thought that she wanted to apologize for herself. Seeing the housewife welcomed like an aristocrat used to hurt me. I had the impression that they kissed her hand to make fun of her, to convey to her that they were not of the same world. She had been born in France; she did not speak Russian; but above all she had married a farmer's boy. She, the daughter of George Theodorovitch, the granddaughter of the mayor of Koursk, became the wife of a *mujik*'s son! That's what they thought. Mummy had no inkling. She found them very distinguished.

'I really don't like being kissed on the hand.'

'But this isn't just any kiss, darling . . . '

He observes me for a moment. He digs around in one of the pockets of his trenchcoat and takes out a parking ticket.

'Here is my home number. I await your call. Make it soon!'

The Mercedes moves off like the wind.

As I passed in front of the Fever again, I was levitating.

The memory plays cruel tricks. From my evening with the writer, I only remember that jibe: 'You're not a novelist as far as I know.' I am still wounded by it.

'You're not a novelist . . . ' What does he know? My French teacher used to read out my homework to the class; she called me 'the literary type'. At fifteen I began a cop thriller, *The Ivory Statuette*. The plot unfolded in Madrid. I had written to the Spanish tourist office to send me a map of the capital. Out of concern for the truth, I had asked the local tobacconist to give me the brand names of Spanish cigarettes. My hero smoked Ducados. At sixteen I perpetrated a collection of poems. *The Song of Tears* appeared in a Burgundian review, the only one which allowed me to publish them at its own expense. I was hoping for letters from readers who had been won over; there were none whatsoever. That drained me of my lyricism. A diary followed it. I would write it every evening before dinner. Into it I slid dried flowers ('Madame Ploquin showed me the passionflower which covers her garden wall. A very Christian plant which conceals the instruments of Our Lord's passion in its corolla: the crown of thorns, the spear, the cross, the scourge, the hammer and the nails'), some cinema tickets ('saw *West Side Story* with Alain. He took me by the hand just when Tony is climbing a metal ladder up to the window of Maria's bedroom'), some birds' feathers, the John Player packet of my first cigarette. I filled three

54

notebooks. Before leaving for Paris, I took them down to the cellar, sheathing them in plastic wrapping to prevent them from being spoilt.

There was no 'Parisian journal'. The letters to my parents, to my girlfriends who had stayed there, made up for this. I stopped writing for pleasure. Until my encounter with the writer.

Did he see anything apart from provocation in my little piece? When, as the scene became clear, the words came in a rush and I subdued them, I rediscovered the feeling of power which had seized me the evening I read like an adult for the first time.

I was ten years old. I devoured adventure yarns, travel stories. Alexandre Dumas, Paul Féval and Tabarly. Books for boys. 'The Green Library'. 'Fifteen Tales of . . . ' All of Jules Verne.

At nine o'clock in the evening I lit the candlestick, set in a lamp. The light brought out the contours of the room. The folds of the curtains lengthened into organ pipes. There I was in Captin Nemo's cabin. I was glancing through his ship's log by the warmth of the stove. I was pronouncing each word out loud, occasionally stopping to observe a diver moving cautiously forward over the sand, through the porthole. I was ten years old. I liked reading but at school I read poorly. My report was more specific: 'Laboured reading. Must try hard.' I kept trying. Every evening in bed I would pronounce the words 'loudly and clearly', as my teacher recommended. I applied myself. I didn't skip over any difficult word; God knows there are enough of them in *20,000 Leagues Under the Sea*. I had reached Chapter 18, page 184 in the 1928 Hachette edition, a first prize of my father.

It was a squid of colossal dimensions, being eight metres in length. It was watching with its enormous, unblinking, glaucous eyes. Its eight arms or rather feet, planted in its head, which have earned the name of cephalopod for these animals, were twice as large as its body and writhed like the hair of the Furies. The two hundred and fifty suckers, laid out on the inner face of the tentacles in the form of semi-spherical capsules, could be distinctly seen . . . Its variable colour which would change with an extreme rapidity according to the animal's irritation, went from being greyish-blue to reddish-brown.

Incredible! I read this passage in less than thirty seconds. I read without reading. The words capitulated from within. They revealed their meaning to me without my pronouncing them. This was magical. Someone was reading for me! I thought I had swallowed another voice.

The strangest thing occurred the next day.

On waking up, I noticed that I had left the lamp on all night. I must have been sleeping restlessly; my nightshirt, hitched up around my waist, was all bunched up. What had prompted me to sit down against the padded bedhead, to take out a small, plastic mirror from the drawer of my night table, to place it between my parted thighs? I was looking inside my fanny for the first time. I examined myself closely like a scientist hunched over his microscope, like the Canadian sailor who followed the unhurried ballet of the octopus through the portholes of the *Nautilus*.

My fanny reminded me of the animal. The same reddish-brown, it was made not of suckers, but of numerous skins folded one over another like the convolutions of lambs' brains.

Moist, somewhat sticky, they had the smell of the sea.

Would I have had the courage to look between my thighs if an inner voice had not been revealed to me the day before? I felt the strength which comes from a new secret. I knew I had been invested with a new power. I had a right to read words without speech; a right to look at my fanny without shame.

'Cooee!'

Catherine always comes in without knocking, her bottle of Four Roses bourbon in her shoulder bag. Kentucky Straight bourbon, *six years old, for the twenty-four-year-old lonely girl*. Catherine turns up when she isn't expected. She suddenly appears with shadows under her eyes, with too much lipstick on her mouth. A sad clown with the body of a star. Catherine is all legs, all eyelashes which she thickens with two layers of mascara. She wears a felt hat like Garbo. She smokes Craven A, only drinks bourbon. She imagines she is a film-maker. For the moment, she is a trainee editor. She often calls on me after the 'rushes'.

'Oh, I must tell you . . . '

She scarcely takes the time to sit down, ferrets about in the studio for an ashtray. She opens the bottle of bourbon, I place two glasses on the carpet. We settle down cross-legged. She lights a Craven A, frowns as she sucks in her first drag: this is her way of introducing a story.

'Yesterday, I went out with a guy who was nice but who could not have been more clinging. You know what I mean . . . '

She drinks a mouthful and carries on with her customary seriousness: 'First of all we saw a movie. Awful. He thought it was "great". He was on the way out. Even so, I asked him home for a drink. At midnight, he still hadn't left. Impossible to get rid of him. *Monsieur* wanted to finish the evening in my arms! I can't stand being smothered in kisses but I let myself be fiddled with. Out of tiredness. The day on the rushes had exhausted me. He began to caress my neck. I wasn't reacting. He concluded that I liked it. I remained inert. I didn't even raise my back to help him take off my jeans. You should have seen him scurrying about my body! He made me think of a mechanic who isn't managing to find the cause of a breakdown. I restrained myself from laughing. At a certain point I felt sorry for him. I told him that I didn't want him but that he could go ahead if he wished. He pulled such a face!'

How I enjoy gazing at her quivering body, her voluble hands! The melancholic clown gives way to the storyteller.

'At which, I lay down on my bed . . . I'll mimic the scene for you.'

She removes the cushions from the divan and stretches out on it, her legs together. She continues with her eyes closed, a Craven A between her lips: 'He pounced on me . . . '

She opens one eye: 'An average sort of weight. You know what I mean . . . I saw what was going to happen right down to the last detail as if I were viewing rushes for the umpteenth time. He tugged at my breast, made a beeline for my clitoris. He clearly wanted to do things properly. I sighed a few times so as not to be beastly. He came shortly afterwards. I was telling myself that he would take his leave at last, that he would pack himself off. But no! He lingered, rubbed himself against my sides, kissed my breasts. And do you know what he came out with?'

She props herself up on her forearm. The low neckline of her pearl-grey blouse reveals deep salt cellars.

' "Oh la la, your fanny is so nice and warm!" Nice and warm! Nice like the brioches in the croissant shops. Tasty! Yum! Yum! Warm like the rolls which the wife of Yvan Iakovlevitch had baked every morning – Have you read *The Nose* by Gogol? I'll give it to you! – melting like those round loaves into which the finger sinks to dig out the soft white crumb. Nice and warm! Your fanny!'

Catherine sits down and passes a hand through her cropped hair.

'You cannot imagine my disgust. Contemplating his air of the satisfied kid who has stuffed himself on sweets after ten days of dieting, feeling my fanny, soft and mushy as a marshmallow teddy bear. I wanted to throw up. He revolted me. I loathed myself. But the worst thing about it, Elisa, the worst thing about it, was that I came in a fever. I really came in a fever,' she repeats, biting her lip.

She pours herself a second glass of bourbon, takes a mouthful, hiccoughs, chokes. The spirit spills over the carpet.

'Oh, sorry! You will reproach me once again for drinking too much!'

I like Catherine. Her genuineness moves me. Her honesty towards herself. She casts a pitiless look over her life, her love affairs. She doesn't delude herself. She wants to see herself as she is. Here she is: cropped hair, extremely thin (Catherine only nibbles at chips, raw carrots and *palmier* cakes) and those endless jeans under which she conceals perfect legs; as if her thirst for truth had led her to mutilate herself.

She watches the bourbon soak into the tightly-woven knots of the carpet.

'Oh, men! It's impossible to find a single one who can make love without claiming that he loves you. They irritate me begging for their ration of tenderness!'

'All of us need it . . . '

In return for such a flat reply, she darts a savage look at me.

'Of course. I'm the first one to admit it. But I don't say to the first guy who comes along that I adore him. I don't sicken my partners with amorous titbits. You can't fuck any longer without the guy declaring he's in love.'

'Does that bother you?'

'It prevents me from coming.'

'But last night . . . '

'Yesterday, the guy was repulsive . . . whence the

orgasm. Anyway enough of all that! Let's talk about Samuel Fuller. I've brought some press cuttings on his last film.'

Catherine is wonderful! If I had faith in women's friendship, if I were convinced that we could say to one another without lying what Montaigne proclaimed of La Boétie: 'Because it was him, because it was me,' I would give her my soul. Catherine would offer me hers in the same surge of abandonment. Friends for life. Impossible. The writer was telling the truth. I have no idea what acid corrodes friendship between women. I suspect several types of it: narcissism, jealousy, a narrow-mindedness which means that instead of thinking, one calculates; instead of liking, one appraises.

Catherine rummages in her bag; her silver bracelets are jangling around her wrists. Despite her thinness, she still has the chubby fingers of a child. I want to slap her for affecting me so much! I lift my glass.

'Pour me out what's left in the bottle. I have to be on form this evening.'

'A new one?'

'No, neither a new one, nor an "ex". Just a friend. A psychoanalyst from Savoie.'

Catherine bursts out laughing.

'You and your intellectuals! You'd better relax, the evening is going to be hard work! I'm off. We'll talk about old Fuller another time.'

Catherine left me her bottle, empty.

'My' psychoanalyst is waiting for me in front of a glass of tequila. I say 'my' as a joke. Because we came across each other in Delphi at the foot of the oracle and he believes he is condemned to love me, he takes great care not to analyse me. His practice is enough for him. I am not keen to lie down on his couch.

When he leaves his native Savoie once a month to

attend a seminar, we meet up at this Brazilian restaurant. I enjoy spicy food, him and samba tunes.

He appears worried. He offers me a badly shaved cheek, then a package trimmed with a ribbon. I unfold the mauve silk scarf by 'Karine of Paris', put it back in its paper and thank Jacques with a quick kiss on his neck.

'What a privilege!' he says in an acidic tone before asking me, as though he were issuing an ultimatum: 'Tequila or whisky?'

'Tequila. What's got into you that you're so tense? Didn't your seminar go well?'

I am infinitely patient with him. I am fond of Jacques. He is bursting with plans: to compile a dictionary of Himalayan dialects for those with the trekking bug, to organize free counselling in psychoanalysis, to write an essay on education. He speaks several languages. He has gone round the world. He knows so much! That is why I am fond of him.

'I can't bear my father's death. You know how much he meant to me. Last week, I left my flat in Chambéry to move into his south-facing house. I have grouped my consultations together over three days. The rest of the week I stay on my own. I prepare my seminars, I read, I look after the vegetable garden. Daddy was not a little proud of it! Shortly before he died, he was thinking about putting in a few tomato plants. This I have done. I feel like an old wolf. Isolation has made me more impassive rather than more sensitive. I harden myself to endure my solitude and I hide my feelings as one hides a shameful deed . . . This morning I was happy. I was going to see you. Once a month; it's not much. I left the house at dawn to catch the first train. I crumbled some bread on the kitchen windowsill and beneath the white lilac; I like the company of birds. Before padlocking the entrance gate, I looked back towards the low façade. I was born in that workman's house, as solid as a rock. Were I ever to have children, I should like it to be between those walls of stone. I'm telling you all this so that you can get to know me.'

I was expecting this sort of talk; he looked so distraught when I saw him coming in. I really do not want to play nursemaid this evening. I point to his steaming plate.

'Your *carreteiro* will get cold.'

He pokes his fork in the minced meat and rice before pushing it away.

'I hunger after your smile, your warmth,' he says in a deep voice while I breathe in coral prawns flavoured with coconut milk, suck the insides of their heads, sprinkle the rice with cassava powder, my cheeks flushed by the heat of the spices.

'I wanted to ring you this week to find out how you were getting on. It is not through indifference that I didn't, on the contrary. Give me your hand.'

I wipe my fingers on the paper napkin, sighing. He seizes my hand: 'Yesterday I took on a new patient. I thought I was dreaming, she looked so much like you. She was a small brunette. She was lively and plump-looking like you; although longer and paler than yours, her face still radiated childhood. Dimples would appear when she smiled, like yours do. The session commenced. Distracted by the memory of you, I was hardly listening to her. Soon your image was superimposed on her body. You were there within distance of my touch, my breath . . . I had to break off the session. That had never happened to me before. Why aren't you saying anything? Stop looking at me like that, your fine airs intimidate me. I happen to have grown up in potato fields!'

I gently withdraw my hand. Every time the scene is the same. Our meetings disappoint me. I would prefer him to talk about his seminar, to lecture me on Lacan rather than harp on that he is attracted to me but that I am too good for him. He gazes at me wearily. He pours himself another glass of Beaujolais. He has finished the entire bottle himself. He sprawls over the table, strewn with crumbs of bread. By trying to lean towards me, he upsets his glass. I lift up the tablecloth in time.

'Jacques, what's going on? My word, you're drunk!'

'No I'm not, I'm in love! In love! Hasn't that ever happened to you? Why don't you love me? Because I've kept my drawling accent, because I have the lumpy hands of common people? I'm proud of them! I didn't choose psychoanalysis to escape my origins, whatever you may think.'

Past midnight. The restaurant is almost empty. Only one couple remains, eating in silence next to us. The young woman with iconic eyebrows throws me furtive looks. My indifference disconcerts her.

'I'm a peasant, is that it? You can't love me without lowering yourself?'

I stand up. He makes me sit down again roughly.

'Hear me out and stop putting on that stuffy air. You must understand me, I'm thirty-two years old. I have had enough of cheap affairs, of experimental affairs, of those between friends, of those with no future. I have had enough of loving for one night. I want to love for life.'

'Let go of me! You're boring me! You're as serious as a judge when you're drunk.'

'Serious! How can one talk of love without being serious!'

Jacques's exclamation has the owner out of the kitchens. He points to his wrist-watch; his establishment is going to close. I indicate that he should bring the bill. He places it near Jacques. I snatch it up. Jacques watches me sign the cheque. He appears to have calmed down.

The night-time bustle of the Halles soothes his agitation. The eccentric dress of the passers-by keeps him amused. He looks back at each of them. He tells me that he would go to classes in ethnology if he had the time. ' "Looks and libido", a good subject for a thesis, don't you think? I already have a few ideas on the topic. Can we discuss them at your place over a coffee?'

I don't have the courage to say no. His train leaves in only an hour's time. What would he do, alone, in the departure hall of the Gare de Lyon?

The five floors got the better of him. Jacques is too fat. The slightest effort leaves him breathless. As a child he was asthmatic. He is not very talkative about his past, as though he were afraid of reviving suffering. His father is exempt from the silence. But he can't call him to mind without a mask of tragedy becoming stuck to his face.

No sooner has he arrived in my studio than he collapses on a chair. I show him the divan.

'Relax there instead. I'll make a coffee. You'll have to excuse me but I only have instant.'

Why did I plant a kiss on his neck before going to the kitchen? Out of kindness? To be forgiven for my sarcastic remarks? He had laid bare his love, while I was feasting on shellfish cooked in a *court bouillon* without condescending to look up at him. He had had the strength to confront my coldness. He played fair, something I never do; for fear of losing.

I didn't hear Jacques come in.

'Why did you kiss me? In the restaurant you were being stuck up. Here you're making eyes at me!'

'I'm not!'

'Yes you are. You've been doing nothing else since the beginning of the evening. Does it amuse you to give me an erection? D'you want to fuck?'

He grasps my bottom so violently that I let go of the sugar bowl. Blue crumbs all over the tiled floor.

'Fool, look what you've . . . '

'Give me your mouth, give me your mouth.'

His frenzy accentuates his grating voice; words scrape his throat. He pins me against the fridge with

one hand, with the other he holds my chin by my jaws.
I turn my head away. He is searching for my lips. His
breath reeks. Unable to break free, I spit in his face. He
backs off.

'Dirty bitch! Bloody nymphomaniac! You still love
your father! Even so, you ought to know that your
Dad's castrated, that you'll never go to bed with him.'

He hurls himself at me again, like a bull charging at
the *muleta*. There can be no doubt: I'm not any
woman but The Woman. If he succeeds in having me,
he will have taken his revenge on the women of the
Creation.

I arch up to block his hand which is clawing its way
through. I resist with every fibre, clenching my fists,
my thighs. A simulacrum of rape. I love it!

'My new panties! You've torn them!'

I knee him in the stomach.

He curls up grimacing, then he screams: 'I'm an ape,
that's what you think, isn't it? Good God say it! Say
that I raped you!'

His cock is peeping out through his half-open fly. A
tip of flesh. A nose. Cyrano. I burst out laughing.

'Poor cunt.'

Jacques is one of those people whom swearing
calms. He turns round slightly to do up his fly. I am
waiting for him to leave, my panties in my hand. He
searches for a final insult as a parting shot. Not finding
one, he snatches my panties out of my hand and
throws them to the ground, just as an officer, wounded
in his pride, would throw down the gauntlet.

I abandon myself to the sunshine, behind the window, with a sky-blue towel tightly wrapped round my bust. This morning the studio has the strange calm of an empty stage. Yesterday's performance was a failure. Jacques and I played our parts badly. Exit Jacques. The only thing he leaves me is a mauve scarf which I will never wear. I dislike its colour. Had it been red, I would have tied it under a blouse, like the writer.

My thoughts are always leading me to him. I almost recounted my affair in the Brazilian restaurant. But Jacques would have flung at me: 'Always in pursuit of the ideal father!' with the irony of the rejected lover which is so biting. Coming from him it would have been a cliché; only coming from him.

When, on waking up, I concluded from the rays of light which were falling on the window that spring had finally arrived, I leapt out of bed. I could have undertaken anything. Fine days stirred up my audacity.

For an hour now I have been fiddling with the parking ticket on which the writer has noted down his phone number. For an hour I have been delaying the moment, minute by minute, when I call him. I am afraid of being awkward. Hearing him is going to make me stammer and without wanting to, I will adopt my mother's shrill tone of voice when she speaks to people whom she suspects are important.

I grab hold of the receiver and dial the number in a great hurry. He answers on the first ring. He must have been writing at his desk.

'How wonderful to hear you, Elisa! I had given up hope. When do we see each other?'

I don't know whether I'm disturbing him or whether he always talks in this rapid way on the telephone. In a faltering voice I beg him to forgive me for ringing at this hour of the morning.

'Your timing couldn't have been better. I have a preview in the late afternoon. To go there by myself is not very appealing. De Kooning, who painted *Women*, does that tempt you?'

I murmur a scarcely audible 'yes'.

'Six o'clock at Beaubourg, at the foot of the escalator. I adore you!'

He rings off.

Dispatched like a common groupie! He might have had the thoughtfulness to find out how I was. He didn't let me get a word in. He just managed to say his piece before hanging up on me.

What did I hope for? For him to lose himself in fine words? I must choose between a Jacques who talks to say nothing and him who says nothing for fear of talking. The choice is made.

I do not go to previews. If it has often happened that in the course of my strolls around Saint-Germain I have passed in front of galleries which were organizing one, I have never ventured in. The feeling that I was committing an offence would have come over me. I would have been unable to enjoy the *petits fours* and the champagne without thinking that I was being sized up by those happy few.

In fact, nobody observes anybody else but themselves. Art lovers who have come for the paintings are rare. The writer is one of those. He cuts a fine figure in a white suit. With his hands behind his back, his body frozen in concentration, he examines each picture. He screws up his eyes, walks up to them, draws back bumping into a group of three women, quickly apologizes to them. He is completely caught up in the painter's turbulent visions.

'Superb! Were he blind, De Kooning would use the same colours. You can sense an unerring command of colour with him. You can feel that even more in his pastels. A pity that there are none of them in the exhibition. I discovered them last year in New York . . . It was magnificent the way he had of crushing chalk.'

'You seem to know a lot about it.'

'I've painted the odd thing . . . If you're good, I'll show you.'

'Is it abstract?'

'Abstract! Art is beyond categorization! I like De Kooning because he can't be classified.'

'The author of the catalogue talks about abstract expressionism . . . '

'Because he has to say something! Because that's what he's paid for! Because if he didn't say it, somebody else would. And if he were to be replaced, what would he be, nothing! Nothing! It's hot in here, don't you think? Wait for me there, I'm going to look for two glasses of champagne.'

My eyes follow him. Strange that nobody has said hallo to him. One canvas makes me stop. *Women in the Country*. Rings of green around watery eyes, coloured mouth: Catherine, the tragic puppet. *Woman in Landscape IV*. No question, it's me. Me after making love, flattened by the pleasure, naked, stiff, beneath squirts of multi-coloured sperm.

The writer returns offering me a glass full to the brim. I point out the painting to him, getting ready to say how much I recognize myself in this dazed woman. He doesn't let me open my mouth.

'What luminous flesh! It is not without reason that De Kooning is compared to Rubens. I would add Goya.

In De Kooning as in the Spanish painter, there is a holy dread of the flesh; one is puritanical, the other . . . What's the matter, Elisa? You seem annoyed?'

I'm not going to make a scene. Wouldn't I be wronging a writer by reproaching him for being prolix?

'Let's leave.'

'Does this fashionable set make you ill-at-ease?'

'A little bit. I don't feel very comfortable among these elegant women.'

I point to a redhead who is rippling in a sheath of crêpe.

'She's all skin and bones! I think you're far more beautiful!'

Beautiful! I take the word smack in the face! Beautiful! 'Morning Radiance' face powder spread over, night cream, eye shadow, lipstick and blusher which heightens the cheekbones, smudged on. Beautiful, I would be truly if I were able to do without creams and make-up. I never go out without it. Like my mother. She would make herself up as soon as she was awake. When she visited her sisters-in-law, she made herself up with greater care. It was her way of showing them that she was not from the country and that although she lived there, she had not relinquished the sophistication of the city dweller. As a child, that shocked me. While finding Mummy more attractive than my aunts, she struck me as dishonest. I resented her for not being like them, for not accepting her lines, for playing 'the lady' when she wasn't a real one.

I too fear not being up to it. Not being beautiful enough. If people assure me that I am, I think of my efforts, my tricks.

Beautiful! Imbecilic! Imbeeeee!!!

The writer smiles at me. I would like to scream: 'My body's beautiful? Touch it! It's fake! Feel away, it's stucco! Stain you fingers with my lipstick enriched by vegetable oils – it keeps lips squashy. Cover your hands with blots of "Deep Black" mascara which gives me the eyelashes of a Nepalese girl. Caress my skin rubbed every morning with a massage glove! Spectator, admire the fine work before you!'

I merely shrug my shoulders.

'You're just saying that to please me.'

He steps back, almost angry.

'Just be a little bit more simple! For heaven's sake, don't stop being the kid I met in the Luxembourg! Why don't you put you pink socks on any more?'

I have dressed up like a vamp to join him. I had my success as I was crossing the Halles. Only he does not appreciate the swaying of my hips, tightly encased in leather, or the roundness of my breasts, which a basque renders more provocative.

'I'm saying that for your own good. You aren't going to follow their pretentious example,' he says pointing to some women draped in soft fabrics. 'Initially they appear very self-assured. They're being the independent woman. But when you mix with them, they "crack", snivel, moan that they no longer "know where they're at". It's so tiresome. Your childlike simplicity seduced me. Don't lose it.'

He is telling the truth: stay simple. Have the frank look of the girls on the collective farms, whose plaits are wound in tight loops on their heads. Have the full cheeks, the round limbs of those girls in shirtsleeves, corn up to their waists, forefingers pointed towards the east. Be positive.

I took him off to the quai Voltaire. Here the light, filtered by the poplars, resembles that on the banks of the Loire. A milky light, blurring the contours, as does the caress of a finger on a charcoal drawing. When I am homesick, it is on the quai Voltaire that I shake myself free of it.

The writer is walking without breathing a word, tearing off branches from the poplars as he goes and breaking them as if to calm an inner seething.

70

'Is it the fact that you had to leave the preview because of me which is making you so gloomy?'

'Absolutely not. I too was feeling stifled . . . '

He falls silent once again.

'How pleasant is it to be out walking with you!'

'How could an old fogey like me amuse you? Above all don't tell me that I don't look my age. Spare me that lie. I'm aware that I'm old. I also realize why you put up with me.'

'Do you now! And why is that?'

'Because I'm a writer.'

Not knowing exactly what reply to make, I mumble that it's not the only reason, that I'm fond of him.

'You're not going to start again!'

He looks at me severely. His left eye starts to wink once more. It makes no difference that I understand it's a nervous tic, it frightens me.

'Elisa, justifying one's feelings distresses me deeply. We are together because this is to our mutual benefit. Mine, you know: you are serving as the model for my book. As for yours, I can guess . . . Let's stop this futile conversation. I don't know why, but I'm feeling better. I even feel quite ready to listen to you.'

'That's unfair! Why should I open my heart to a man who refuses to do the same for me!'

'Because your character fascinates me, whereas in my case, I don't interest you as an individual but as a writer. Don't deny it. The interest which you have in me – if at all – is narcissistic. I act as your mirror. I am used to it and I like it. So, talk away! Tell me for example why you suggested that we go down to the quai Voltaire.' I sigh. 'Tell me. Speak to me. Talk away.'

It is by recounting memories that they are spoilt. Should one attempt to, they appear less striking, like butterflies which when clumsily caught, lose their pigments by leaving a little wing dust on the fingers.

If I tell the writer that the Seine, by the quai

Voltaire, reminds me of the Loire, he will laugh in my face. If I add that the poplars remind me of my mother, he will stare wide-eyed.

In September, Mummy and I would go blackberry picking. We cycled off, a basket fixed to the rack. With her excessive delight, the shrill cries she gave when we hurtled down a hill, Mummy made me think of a convalescent for whom this was the first outing. She had left my father at home, she who normally did nothing without him. When I reproached her for lacking independence, she retorted that husband and wife are never apart. This attitude weighed her down without doubt, for how otherwise explain her euphoria whenever we absconded? She marvelled at everything: the stillness of the road, the austere beauty of the harvested fields and above all, the golden tinge of the poplars which she would say 'had put on their best clothes to greet the autumn'.

We set our bicycles down on the verge. The birds, which were gathering blackberries, would fly off at our approach. Sometimes one of them, more daring, stayed beside us to pinch the fruit which we were taking from the bush with precise pecks of its beak. Mummy would laugh. How I loved her then! The black juice ran down our lips. We licked our fingers. Mummy didn't scold me for having stained my dress; the blackberries had fallen on hers as well.

During these moments, Mummy slipped free of my mother. Another person emerged, light of heart. During these moments, I was no longer the flesh of her flesh. Neither mother, nor daughter, nor family existed. Neither duty nor fault. Liberty has the acidity of red fruit.

'I brought you to the quai Voltaire to relax. Water has a calming influence . . . '

'It's not having much effect on you. You strike me as

even more tense than at the preview. I have the impression that you haven't taken in what I have said.'

'What have you said? Ah! The thing about the mirror! My narcissism! If only you knew how totally indifferent I am to it!'

'No, little girl, quite the reverse. You're its prisoner. You have taken such care with your image . . . I'm beginning to know you. You feel an irresistible need to be attractive. To attract everybody. I would almost say anybody at all, provided you come away with an even more flattering image of yourself. The writer I am was the classic prey for this nymphomaniac's seduction.'

'You're out of line! Leave me alone! Let me go!'

'Wait, I haven't finished.'

I don't hear anything any more. The tears are welling up in my eyes. To be attractive! Attractive! That's what's at stake! If I'm not, I die. So why have I grown up? It was so simple then. 'Little girl', he called me 'little girl'. But it's over, it has gone wrong, it won't come back. I am a woman, a woman who cries for wanting to be so attractive.

'Elisa, I don't know what to say . . . Elisa. I let myself get carried away. Here, dry your tears.'

He offers me a handkerchief of finely hemstitched cambric, trimmed on each corner with a triangle of lace. He, blow his nose on this foppery! Examining it, I notice an embroidered monogram. He snatches it out of my hands.

'I'm not going to eat it!'

'It's the only memento of my mother I have left.'

The mystery thickens. The image of the little countryman and that of the writer were not easily superimposed; that of the refined farmer's wife appears yet more unusual. But what is the point of telling lies over a handkerchief?

'Your mother liked beautiful things . . . '

'Of course. Don't talk about her to me any more. Forgive me for leaving you so abruptly. I'm about to be a little unfaithful to you. Rue Solferino.'

Let him go, it's better this way.

I prepare to turn and go back; he stops me.

'Elisa, I resent myself for saying those stupid things.'

'It's all forgotten.'

'I have to make amends to you.'

'You don't have to at all!' I retort, my arms firmly crossed over my bust, my head held high as I imitate the pose of those pioneering Soviet women, whom I have promised myself I will resemble.

'You must go, you'll be late.'

He tosses me a kiss and moves off. When he quickens his pace, his lopsidedness gives him a slight limp.

Recognizing the same face, always the same, when, from a distance, a bearded man is moving along; the same silhouette behind every trenchcoat, every grey and black suit. Starting at the sight of a spiral notebook or an embroidered handkerchief which a woman takes out of her bag.

I see him everywhere. Not a man passes by who does not make me think of the writer, one for his blue eyes, another for the scarf which, like him, he ties beneath his shirt. This one because he is writing on the terrace of a café; that other who is savouring a cocktail.

I spotted the suit he was wearing in the Luxembourg in one of the windows of Old England, the shop on the boulevard des Capucines. I went in. A shop assistant advanced towards me. I asked him whether the material for the suit on display with the raincoats in the last-but-one window was indeed Prince of Wales check. In an amiable voice he affirmed this to be so. When I wanted to know whether he sold much of it, the look on his face froze over. He replied that this model was very popular. His curt tone didn't discourage me. Determined to discover the writer's identity, I wasn't going to shrink from any ruse, however clumsy. As a pretext I said that I was conducting a sociological survey for a fashion magazine. I therefore had to find out to which socioprofessional categories Prince of Wales check appealed; whether it attracted artists, notably writers..I was talking at great speed: my lie struck me as being so poor that I was anxious to finish it. The shop assistant seemed to be paying more attention to my appearance than to what I had been saying. 'I really have no time to satisfy that sort of request. Speak to the supervisor.' Half smiling, he added that he could none the less lend me a biro and pad for taking notes. I cast a glance at the back of the shop. The supervisor was standing in front of the cashmere pullovers. He was a fine-looking man of around sixty. His stiff bearing was distinctly unpromising. I announced to the shop assistant that I had left my questionnaire in the car.

As I left, I was seized by a fit of giggles. The spasms which filled my throat were more like sobs.

It was diseased, thinking so much about him. Shameful. What had happened to my offhandedness? I didn't know what attracted me to him. Only his shortcomings struck me: his self-importance, changes of mood, obsession with flaunting his culture, peremptory affirmations: 'I don't interest you as an individual. I serve as your mirror. Your nymphomaniac's seduction,' the way he took himself seriously. All that irritated me. Yet I hoped for only one thing: to see him again. The adventure was taking a ludicrous turn but like a television serial, I wanted to discover how things ended.

I spent two hours in a large bookshop in Saint-Germain, in the hope that I would unearth one of his novels from among the hundreds of works. The shop assistants of the Divan quickly spotted this girl who was turning over the volumes in the 'new publications' stack one after another without opening a single one.

I skimmed through the biographies of authors printed on the backs of jackets, hunting down villages in Normandy, peasant childhoods; scant traces. I cursed editors who considered the novelist's photo to be superfluous; they were reducing my chances of finding the emaciated face with its gash of a faunlike smile. The reproductions of paintings on glossy covers led me into a silent hide-and-seek. Was I overheated in front of this self-portrait by Van Gogh? The resemblance, though vague, was misleading me. Would he have found this drawing by David Hockney appealing? Picasso? Tiepolo? He liked Mignard and allegorical frescoes. Philippe de Champaigne? Would he have picked this nude by Egon Schiele whose furious pencil strokes were reminiscent of De Kooning? The Dutchman was one of his favourite painters. According to my researches, none of his canvases had served as a cover for a novel.

I went from one book to another, hesitating in front of a Goya etching, instinctively dismissing a labyrinth by Escher. When I noticed the portrait of Mademoiselle Rivière, I thought I had reached my goal. At our first encounter, the writer had referred to Ingres; in his view, my neck would have inspired him. I had interpreted this remark as flattery aimed at me, when in fact it was a tribute intended for the painter. My elation was shortlived. The portrait illustrated an essay in psychoanalysis. I was growing weary. I didn't have the courage to fathom the interminable charade of the titles. One alone caught my eye just as I went through the automatic doors . . . *Where the Cattle Drink*. It was surely with these animals that the writer shared his desire to escape? I imagined the scene in a field with a stream running alongside. When I saw 'tragi-comedy' written in the finest of lettering beneath the title, I put the volume down again; the writer was not a playwright.

These fruitless investigations have drained me. I struggle forward, suffocating in a hounds-tooth suit, dressed like Lauren Bacall: tight waist, shoulders widened by felt padding sewn into the armholes of the jacket, my bust accentuated by darts fitted in a high position. The likeness stops there. Lauren wouldn't twist her ankles every ten steps, she wouldn't readjust her skirt, nor sniff, she wouldn't have this face crumpled by disappointment. Anger would be irradiating her features.

Bogart has deceived her. He prepares to raise anchor, when only the day before he promised to take her on board with him. Bacall learns this through a ship's boy in love with her. She races towards the harbour in a soft-top. Having set foot on his old tub, she slaps the hero, who slaps her back. She slaps him again. He takes her aboard. Happy end.

I ought to act in the same way. I have showed myself to be too conciliatory, refraining from contradicting him, offering only feeble protests against his sarcastic remarks, preferring that he regard me as a simpleton rather than displease him. This diplomacy of the coward can but try him the more. A thrashing, that's what he deserves. I'm going to mete it out to him straight away! It will give me back my honour and present him with a new scene for his novel.

What sort of novel is he writing for me to be its main character? I cannot lay claim to the beauty of Emma; I am older than Gigi; I have neither the raillery of Zazie, the depth of Eugénie, nor the pride of Mathilde . . .

I am reflecting in this way as I go down the rue Bonaparte, when a shop brings me to a halt: some autographs, some letters of politicians and writers are on display behind the window. I hold vengeance in my grasp.

I walk off to isolate myself in a café.

Mr Writer,

I cannot call you anything else, not knowing your name. I wasted my afternoon trying to ascertain it. In vain. However I described you to the shop assistants of a large bookshop – 'He's slim. He has a pepper-and-salt beard. His eyes are light. He only smokes cigarillos' – their faces appeared perplexed. You must admit it's odd. Your name would scarcely matter if you agreed to talk to me about your novels. But I am deprived of that too. In all likelihood you are no more a writer than I am . . . I could go on with my investigation but I have wasted enough time. That is why before you exhaust the novelistic springs of my personality, I am setting you free as from now. I am leaving you. The expression is laughable. It suits lovers better than strangers who have been playing at cat and mouse. But it is the only thing you can do when somebody no longer interests you. Have no fear for your novel; heroines are unique but their models interchangeable.

Goodbye, Artist!

On rereading it, my letter strikes me as sententious. But what is done, is done. I buy an envelope in a tobacconist's.

A spiral staircase leads to the small room in the Fever. Six o'clock. The bar is empty. Only client, the bald man in the black polo-neck sipping a cocktail absent-mindedly. Robert scarcely displays any more energy. Leaning against a shelf on which bottles of spirits are lined up, you can't tell whether he is meditating or dozing. At my approach, he stands up straight and gives me a routine smile. He hasn't recognized me. That is hardly surprising. I came here only once. However good his memory for faces is, how could he guess that this young woman in a suit and the little girl who had behaved temperamentally over a cup of tea are one and the same person? By the glances I am throwing around the room, he concludes that I have a date and asks me whether I am waiting for someone. I shake my head and offer him the envelope.

'Whom do you want me to hand it to? There's no name!'

'I don't know the addressee's name. He invited me here two weeks ago. He was wearing a check suit that day.'

'Listen, you're charming but I don't examine the suits of all the customers. What does your gentleman look like?'

I repeat the description I have given the booksellers. He says that he can't remember.

'But heavens above, he's a writer!'

'A writer, a writer! You must be kidding! The Fever is full of people who write. The little bald fellow at the far end, he's one and a good one at that!'

Robert takes the greatest of care with his clients, as a trainer does his champions. He reserves their tables, takes their messages, inquires discreetly after their affairs, their health and doesn't hesitate, if one of them is doing too much credit to his cocktails, to point this out to him. He knows he is indispensable.

'Sorry I can't be more useful to you. Here's your envelope back.'

'Wait! I also know that he only drinks remsem coolers.'

'Thanks for the information. It's the star drink of the Fever. I serve dozens of them every day. I invented it,' he says, emphasizing the middle word. 'The remsem has allowed me to carry off the Golden Shaker at the best barman competition. I would have named it "Robert's cocktail", had the boss agreed . . . '

I maintain that his boss was right; 'Robert's cocktail' doesn't sound good. On the other hand, 'the diabolical Robert' . . .

'The diabolical Robert,' he repeats in enchantment. 'You wouldn't think it but you've got something there. Here, give me your letter.'

'What's the point if you don't know my writer?'

'Of course I do. He even orders a glass of warm water with his cocktail. He often has a sore throat. As you can see, I do know him! But,' he adds, leaning towards me, 'he wants to remain incognito. I won't tell you any more. No point in insisting.'

He wedges the envelope between a bottle of armagnac and white rum.

As I go up the stairs again, I hear him murmuring: 'The diabolical Robert.'

I was caught in my own trap. The writer hadn't lied to me. If he took my letter seriously, it would be the end of our meetings. Farewell heroine! Farewell mirror!

I remained confident, however. The writer had become sufficiently attached to me not to be offended at a letter written on impulse. Moreover, this letter testified to real character.

I marched along the boulevard Saint-Germain like a warrior, victory in my soul, as I had done so many times before.

The boulevard Saint-Germain from the underground at Bac to the stop at Maubert crossed my territory of romance. I have covered it in the early morning, my body made light by a night of love; waltzing around dustbins, smiling at the street sweepers, laughing at myself, at my night cries, the piercing cries of the young she-cat which has been seized by the scruff of the neck. I had left my lover while he slept, as the unfettered woman does. His name was vanishing in the raw air. I strode away. His voice was fading, the contours of his body were growing blurred. By the next day, only a single detail remained: the outline of an arm, a hip.

Of my first boyfriend, I simply recall his hip. The one and only recollection of our love affair which two phrases exchanged in the back row of a classroom initiated. September 1979.

'Do you like Gogol? I have just read *Dead Souls*. Great!'

'We're made to understand each other: I have Russian origins.'

A few centimetres of recording tape snatched from oblivion just like an image: his hip.

How I loved it, the hip of my first boyfriend! Like a child's shoulder-blade, it stuck out in a point when, resembling an Etruscan effigy on its sarcophagus, he stretched out naked at my side. How I would often caress it! My hand moulded the curve scooped out by the hipbone. My hand lingered on his sides, hesitated to descend towards his waist again, then hurried down over his long, knotty thighs.

One could write a novel about what one has loved! I would celebrate that hip with the lyricism which first loves inspire. I would do better to keep silent. I was mistaken. I thought his hip was unique and love eternal. The affair lasted two months; as for his hip . . .

I found it again long afterwards planted on the body of a one-night stand, in the chance course of an erotic position.

An exaggerated concavity, this pointed hipbone: unquestionably it was the same one. I experienced the same egotistical pleasure in caressing it. Coincidence.

'On waking up, Elisa realized that her partner had changed bodies during the night. He had swapped his hip for that of the preceding lover without her knowing either how or why they had negotiated this exchange.'

My lovers have the same flesh. Whether it is Pierre's, Paul's or Jacques's, the body which has clasped me, which I have clasped, assumes its anonymous bulk once again, from the moment that it lies back, slaked, against mine. There is just one flesh: that which is giving me pleasure. My lovers' bodies resemble each other. Yet I track down their differences, as though I were refusing to admit to myself that making love to one boils down to doing the same thing with another. I idealize their bodies. One's languid pose inspires me to a quatrain. I desire that other for his rounded muscles, similar to those of Saint

82

Sebastian of Sodoma.

I am fetishistic in love. As a child I used to collect butterflies and coleopterans, the shells of which I would pierce with a pin so the entrails could ooze out. I filled a cocoa tin with hundreds of glass eyes, gouged out of teddy bears and old dolls.

Their uncommon iridescence would show up under the naked light of a bulb, in front of which I made them gleam.

I label my lovers. I pin them down in my memory. I class them in families of delicate hips, pudgy shoulders, thighs like the shafts of columns, Greek feet, in the same way as that Pope who had ancient statues emasculated and arranged their penises in a *studiolo*, in which he would shut himself up to meditate.

I have chosen to forget the cock which opened me up; those which made me come; those the sperm of which spurted over my stomach; those which hurt me; those I sucked until I was nauseous. Forgotten.

To his place, he's inviting me to his place! In an hour, we'll be drinking champagne in the rue du Temple.

I wasn't expecting him to react so quickly. I handed the letter to Robert yesterday. So he cares for me.

He must be phoning from the Fever. I can hear laughter, crystal-clear sounds with which his voice, by its liveliness, is in harmony.

'Elisa, I've read your letter. What a fright it gave me! For a writer that's a gift, one of those shocks to the system to which Stendhal was partial. Have you read the *Chartreuse*? Hello?'

'I'm listening.'

I can't get over it: he doesn't appear to resent me. Has he guessed that the letter was just a subterfuge?

He called me at home; so he hasn't lost the piece of paper on which I noted down my phone number when we parted at the Val-de-Grace. Perhaps he has always kept it on him?

'A great novel, wouldn't you say? To think that today, feelings make a book suspect! Hello? Why aren't you saying anything? You'll go back on your decision? We are going to see each other?'

'Of course. That letter was a gag. I wanted to pull your leg.'

'You succeeded. My God, what a shock! Robert handed me the envelope, not without ceremony. It's light, unscented. I deduce from this that it isn't from an admirer. Don't snigger. I am able to boast a numerous correspondence with women over their problems. You're the only one . . . Let's return to the letter. "I'm leaving you . . . Goodbye, artist." What a nerve! Not only does she make fun of me but she asserts that my novel won't suffer from her desertion. "Their models are interchangeable." What a cheek! Damnation, I've spilt the remsem over my trousers.'

I'm hardly listening to him. I'm imagining his flat, similar to Freud's. Dark, cluttered up with strange curios: a Venus, some phallic symbols, some primitive gods, Chinese puzzles . . . Books line the walls, are heaped up on the furniture, are strewn over the floor. On the left of a window looking out on to a small courtyard, the table at which he writes. I notice scattered pages on it: his novel. I read my name on one of them.

While I daydream, the writer continues his monologue.

'I curse, I swear. I am twenty. I confuse rage and affection. I don't know whether I should execrate or praise your insolence. I reread your letter: my anger then subsides, just as the storm abates. Your round handwriting, those phrases innocently aligned on a page doubtless torn out of your diary – you do keep one, don't you? – as well as the wide margin which you put in on the right as the conscientious student does: all that moves me. You have acted like the child you still are. Conserve that freshness. It is rare among women of more than twenty.'

'All in all, for you I'm just a specimen.'

'No. You take me back to the past. You remind me of the girls of my adolescence, of those little milkmaids, modest and pert at the same time, whom Proust so accurately portrayed. I'm afraid that Paris may spoil you. We will talk about that at home, dear heroine. I await you.'

'Dear heroine.' Which one? If I put on Ivory foundation, he will nickname me Ophelia. I will play the *ingénue*, fluttering my eyelids, shaded by lilac and vanilla.

'The make-up blends together in a confluence of lilac colouring. With a hint of pink, the clearness of opaline, the delicacy of porcelain, the cheeks are given soft tints using all the artifices of powders and creams, so as to regain the very bloom of innocence.'

Elle, no. 1973, October 1983

Drums and trumpets. Judith *Triumphans*. I'm radiating. I blind those strolling by. As I walk past, they turn round, then their indistinct silhouettes disappear. Their looks converge on me as on the Charioteer of Delphi; all are enraptured: 'How beautiful!' That is what they can say of my body at this actual moment. The exterior is beautiful. But the interior, if only you knew!

The Queen of Sheba of the rue de Rivoli has gone off the rails like an out-of-control machine. Her eyeballs quiver, her intestines ripple, her heart under massive stress pumps out the blood wildly. The cutaneous cells secrete her sweat from her back, armpits and hands. A white woman, subject to flows, places, seasons and winds.

Rue du Temple, I have reached what meteorologists call 'the dew stage', when the mass of air saturated by humidity heralds the storm.

Two modernistic caryatids stand guard over the front door. I'm going to turn to jelly on the red carpet which covers the marble staircase. Top floor. Right-hand door. My thighs are trembling. Jets of blood are pounding my temples. I move forward as an intruder. I raise my hand towards the bell ... Laughter! I heard laughter behind the door. He isn't alone. There is a woman with him, possibly two. I thought I made out two shades of laughter: one spasmodic, the other fuller like a cooing.

Slumped on a chintz sofa in front of a low table on which some glasses filled with an amber drink sparkle, all three stare at me without saying anything. Thin and blonde, the two women appraise me ostentatiously. One of them whispers a remark in the ear of her neighbour. The latter bursts out laughing and leans towards the writer. Yes, that's how it is. He has invited two of his admirers (or mistresses) to a makeshift court. Before I arrived, he announced to them that he wanted to take his revenge on a little girl who had made fun of him, a little girl in whom he had had complete faith. Since nobody can be more cruel than women, he has given them *carte blanche* to carry out the punishment in his place. He has assured them that he will not intervene whatever their ploys, that he will merely admire their finesse.

I no longer hear a sound. The light goes out. I remain in the gloom, hesitating to ring . . .

'What on earth are you doing in the dark!'

The tap-tapping of my stilettos must have informed him of my arrival. He is standing back from the door, his face in the shadows. He appears gigantic to me. The writer. Rooted to the sisal doormat, I contemplate my illusion.

As I enter, I notice that nobody is there. I offer him my hand, relieved. He raises it to his lips, then tells me to make myself comfortable.

The flat is sparsely furnished. Turkish carpets cover the floor and three boxes serve as seats. Opposite a sofa in white leatherette, a long table of polished wood overwhelmed by papers. He writes here by the light of this lamp, he declares, pointing to a hookah topped by a lampshade. He also shows me the Tibetan bowl which acts as his tidy, as well as an immense sago leaf lacquered royal blue. He explains that the pith of this palm tree – sago – an amylaceous substance, a sort of yellowish starch, goes into the food of Indians and Malayans. Evasively I agree. Where is the huge library I was expecting? There isn't a single book, apart from a few tourist guides on a shelf. I comment on this. He laughs and replies that the owner of the flat doesn't read much, though this hasn't prevented him from being his best friend, his only friend, he corrects. He is a photographer. When he leaves on a story, he lends him his two-room flat so that he can write undisturbed.

This is not his flat! I, who was beginning the game of the Chinese portrait! He likes Turkey, Tibet and palm trees. I find it hard to disguise my disappointment. I ask him why he prefers to write at other people's houses rather than his own.

He makes a vague gesture: 'I am at home everywhere! At the Fever, here or elsewhere. It doesn't matter.'

'Where do you live when your friend returns home from his trips?'

'In a hotel. I have no ties in Paris, no ties of any sort, moreover. My only sphere, writing; my only homeland, solitude. I bathe in it, like a foetus in amniotic fluid. As for my umbilical chord, I cut it myself whenever I want,' he says, pulling the telephone chord out of its socket.

He smiles, seeing me start.

'Don't be afraid. I haven't lured you into an ambush.'

He plugs the phone in again and tells me that I can dial 17 at the slightest improper move on his part. There is an immediate ring of the phone. He sighs.

'The importunate flock is bleating once more.'

'You're not answering?'

As the ringing persists, he pulls the phone out wearily. This is the first time that he has betrayed any weakness in my presence. Does he really crave this solitude? Hasn't he just imposed it upon himself to heal a secret wound? I ask him. His look of disdain sweeps over me.

'Spare yourself this tuppenny-ha'penny psychology. I have no "secret wound". I like being alone, although today it's a defect. The recluse reminds me of a leper in the Middle Ages: you avoided him while wondering what dreadful things he could have committed to know this fate. However, without solitude – no creation.

"The poet is like the prince of clouds
Who haunts the tempest and laughs at the archer;
Banished to the ground to a chorus of booing."

'I discovered Baudelaire at fifteen. My youth . . . "a dark storm"!'

I ask him firmly not to deflect the conversation. He sits down on the sofa, lights a cigarillo and says with an ironical air: 'Well, let us continue, *mademoiselle*, if such is your pleasure. What were we talking about exactly? Ah yes, my solitude. It is of interest to you. It inspires compassion in you! It awakens your need to cuddle, to cosset! That bloody maternal instinct which artists die of!'

He draws himself up, one hand clenching the arm of the sofa as though he wanted to contain the fury which is brewing within.

'I was in the embrace of solitude ever since my childhood. I was a proud, anti-social little person. You were too? You must have certain literary gifts: a lonely childhood predisposes one to write. I too kept a diary. I only talked about myself in it; it was very sweet but completely sterile. I very quickly became convinced of this. At fourteen, I declared myself to be a stoic and absolutely agreed with that thought of Marcus Aurelius: "It is shameful that when the mind's strength is drained, the body's endures." A book of maxims followed my journal in which I laid down rules of conduct for myself in writing. "Furnish my life with unity. Don't shrink from the world, action, struggle, anything which develops the will. Don't be afraid of wanting . . . " You're looking at me strangely . . .'

'I was wondering . . . That has got nothing to do with what you were telling me. I was thinking of the chance which brought us together. You, a writer, in search of a model and I . . . '

'Yes . . . '

I don't dare admit that for three days now I have been writing every morning. Short pieces. Some portraits: an old woman from Martinique by whose side I travelled on the underground; the baker's wife, so pale that you expect her to collapse when she holds out your *baguette* to you. I should like to show them to him, seek his advice. I should like him to encourage me. Who else could do it better than him? That is why I want to see him in the future. That I am his heroine, he my mirror or something else, strikes me as ridiculous. Let us stop this game . . .

He has risen to his feet. He motions that I wait for him. He is going to look for the champagne to drink to this chance.

He returns with a magnum and two mustard jars decorated by transfers. He begs me to forgive him for not having any flutes and announces that he has left another bottle to cool.

At the first glass, the champagne seems delicious; at the second, the writer becomes so. I am just about to gulp down the third when he whispers: 'Now my darling, I want to know everything about your love affairs.'

His curiosity makes him puerile. He is wriggling about on the sofa as I myself used to, when Daddy came back on certain evenings with some Swiss chocolate. I had to stay well behaved until the end of dinner for him to give me permission to unwrap the little rectangular bricks, lined up in a cardboard box like a game of dominoes. I was so obedient . . . Why should I be today? I am no longer ten years old.

'That's enough talk about me! I've had enough of playing the heroine! Of playing the dolly!'

'You aren't a dolly. Do you think that I'm interested in you? Come on, finish your glass so that I can bring another bottle. We're going to drink to our friendship.'

The word makes me giggle. I remind him that a short while ago, he considered women incapable of true friendship.

'But you're not like that! Don't take everything I propose as gospel! I'm not a moralist! If I were, who would listen? Morality is no longer fashionable. What do people read these days? Adventure stories, historical novels, spicy confessions. Although my talent doesn't prompt me to undertake the latter, I have let myself be led by my editor. For commercial reasons. One has to live . . . So do be co-operative.'

My head is spinning. I feel slightly drunk. It's not serious. Nothing is. Neither he nor I, neither his past nor mine, my love affairs, my secrets.

'Dear writer, listen well. I'm going to recount my first night of love to you. The word "love" is excessive: I didn't love that boy. I was twenty, I was saying to myself that it was time to take the plunge . . . '

'Don't lose yourself in commentary. Rather, describe his poses. What did he do first when he closed the door? I suppose that it happened at his house.'

'Yes, in his bedroom. He asked me whether I wanted to drink something. As I stayed without moving, he came up to me and pressed his lips to mine.'

'Had he already made love?'

'I suppose so. I didn't care. I told you: I didn't love him. His breath stank of wine. I didn't open my mouth. He then sat down on a stool, his arms folded. I realized that I had to go to it. I got undressed like a big girl . . . '

'Why "like a big girl" ? '

'Why! I've no idea, it's just an expression.'

If I revealed everything, I would tell him that Mummy had greeted my first period with one single remark: 'Now you're a big girl,' then she ordered me to go and change. I took off my panties. I sniffed them surreptitiously before carrying them in my fingertips to the laundry basket. They smelt of hare's entrails, strings of warm flesh which my father, an expert hunter, would carefully remove with the aid of a kitchen knife. Daddy would tell me to stay by his side. He held out the bleeding intestines, while asking me to throw them into the rubbish bin.

'So,' the writer says, 'you got undressed . . . '

'I lay down on his divan covered in downy plush. He in turn meticulously took his clothes off, as though he were alone, slipping his socks into his shoes, putting these away under the radiator side by side, folding his trousers over the back of a mahogany chair, always the same I suppose, obeying those derisory rituals which strike us as completely our own, whereas they are for the most part common to everybody.'

'Stick to the point. Details but no commentary.'

'He turned round to take off his underpants. Then with a serious expression he came towards me, or possibly it wasn't so serious . . . I no longer remember. The machinery was engaged. He caressed my breasts, licked them cagily. I let him do what he wanted. I ran my hands over his back. At a certain moment, he seized them to place them on . . . his balls. I had the impression that I was holding some fruit. I told myself that they were plums. That relaxed me. I was opened up. Easy, everything followed on like the twelve hours of the clock, the twenty-four hours of the day, the three hundred and sixty-five days of the year, the four seasons, the twenty-one-day cycle, the three letters of the word "End", the word "End" at the end of the film. I was those hours, days, letters. I was that end. Declined, recited, gone through, read, experienced, then abandoned. I hadn't felt a thing. The sheets remained unsullied.'

'Little tart!'

I laugh. I tell him that he has drunk too much champagne; I too I may add. I feel tipsy. 'Tipsy!' I really am very merry. So why is the writer pulling that shirty face? 'What a tart.' I continue to laugh.

'Does it amuse you that I call you a tart? Do you like it? Does it excite you? What excites you? Go on, tell me, little tart. Tell me what your pimp does to excite you? What about me? Do I excite you? Tell me, tart! You're not answering. Answer! Do I excite you? But what are you doing? Don't go! Elisa, don't go! I was joking! I was joking! Elisa!'

I rushed down the stairs. 'Tart. Tart.' On the street, the refrain was carrying on louder than ever. The passers-by, they too could hear it. They were going to proclaim it in unison. 'Tart. Tart.' They were going to surround me, accuse me.

Lisbon! What on earth can he be doing in Lisbon?

Lisbon. Lisboa. Flower and snake. Town where everything is rotting, where everything slides. My footsteps slid on the cobblestones of the port, as gleaming as scales. Alone abroad for the first time. I was eighteen. My freedom had the whiff of soap and fried cod.

I reread his telegram.

RETURNING IN A MONTH. WILL EXPLAIN. ABSOLUTE NEED OF YOUR STORIES. SEND THEM TO ME AT THE FOLLOWING ADDRESS: RESIDENSIA INGLESA. RUA DAS JANULAS VERDES. 471200 LISBOA.

YOURS EVER

Rua des Janulas Verdes. A nice area doubtless. In the Rato, behind the Praça Marquês de Pombal. A luxurious hotel. A room darkened by frilly double curtains. A smell of polish and mothballs. He writes on the leather-covered writing leaf of a *commode-secrétaire*. Why has he chosen Lisbon?

And I, why did I pitch up there, a bag over my shoulder, late one afternoon? Autumn had almost arrived. Through the grimy windows of the bus I could see the pale line of buildings on the Avenida Amiramte. It was daylight still but the neon lighting of the transport companies, travel agencies, big hotels and banks was glimmering faintly. In front of their façades palm trees were swaying, wispy as feather dusters. I had hoped for intense excitement, I was plunging into dreariness. Lisbon reminded me of the dining room at home, cramped and gloomy with its bulky furniture. I didn't have room to play when I took refuge in it on rainy days. It would have meant pushing the table towards the window but it weighed such a lot.

Lisbon thus combined narrowness and heaviness. Funny stop for a runaway.

Writers don't abscond, they go into exile. Exile has virtues for whomsoever wants to write. But he who couldn't care less about other places, why Lisbon?

By leaving home, I was finally going to live. That was what I had written in a letter placed on the kitchen table. Mummy would find it going down to make the coffee. I got on the school bus which went by our house at half-past seven. It made a stop at the station; I got out by the door at the back.

I had chosen Lisbon out of cowardice. I had built up such a perfect picture of Venice, London or New York that I was afraid not so much of their disappointing me as of my disappointing them.

When you come to Paris from Anjou, to leave for Lisbon is child's play; at the gare d'Austerlitz I only had to change platforms.

It's decided. I'm going to rejoin the writer.

I had found a room in the Alfama, a working-class area, clinging to the heights. Sitting on the doorstep, my landlady was crocheting a shawl, imitating the *guipures* of Manoeline monasteries. I told her that it was beautiful. That flattered her. She led me towards a bright room. In the drawer of the bedside table, her previous patron had forgotten a sock.

'Hello? North South Travel Agency? I would like to know what time the first train leaves for Lisbon. There's only one a day? It's not important. Nine o'clock. Gare d'Austerlitz, isn't it? And I arrive? Five to ten the next morning at Santa Apolonia station. No, I won't reserve.'

To pass unnoticed through the side steets of the old town, I had dressed in black like the women who trudged along with a beast's heavy tread, always weighed down by bags. My arms swinging, I walked straight ahead, moving from one alleyway to another without hesitation. The men's insistent looks unmasked the foreign girl. They would stare neither at my breasts, nor my arms, nor my mouth; they stared at my legs. Their wives didn't have these sleek, sinewy calves, but short legs on which their stockings flattened an unsightly network of dark hairs. My sleek legs aroused desire in the eyes of the men. A desire of resignation. When they brushed against me, their lips spat out obscenities but their eyes remained melancholic.

'Hello? Don't hang up! One last thing. What's the price of a return ticket? Second-class . . . One thousand and sixty-six francs. While you're there, how much does the excess fare for the sleeper cost? Yes, a single. Two hundred and eighty-one francs the trip. If I want to reserve?'

I followed the first man who spoke to me. He hadn't lusted after my legs. He had smiled as he asked me in gestures if I felt cold, then he had pointed towards the sky with his forefinger and said '*Soon, the rain* . . . 'He was wearing the shapeless suit of Lisbon men, wide trousers, soft jacket. He was ageless like so many men there. He didn't inspire either fear or liking in me. He was alone like me.

We sat down in a café in the Baixa, deserted at this hour. A juke-box provided some *paso doble* tunes. We drank hot chocolate in beer mugs. I followed the liquid's course down my oesophagus; I was warming up through my stomach. The man began by caressing my breasts through my blouse. The only thing I saw was this room tiled in white. He slipped his finger between two buttons, then his hand seized my breast; I felt it harden. I felt the mocking erection of my nipple, the agreeable enough spasm of my clitoris. That made me laugh. *'You love men,'* said the man.

I will spend this afternoon booking seats.

The café was closing. We were asked to leave. After ten o'clock lethargy descends on the town. I had no idea where I was: far from my room, for I could no longer make out the tall cranes of the docks. Far from everything: from my country, my family, my body. I had lost my voice; I couldn't hear anything; I had stopped thinking while the man, who had immobilized me in the corner of the doorway, was gently fingering my crotch. Higher up . . . He had jammed his finger in. The light from a streetlamp was blinding me. I had closed my eyes. He was wanking me off. With my head resting on his scrawny shoulder, I was getting wet. I hummed one of those silly tunes which I used to sing to myself as a child when I had to walk in the dark. I was getting wet. My fanny cried out for joy. A waft of fish cooked in the sun, of cuttle bone rose; my mucous membranes rediscovered their distant marine origins. My fanny smelt of Lisbon. I was that proud, weary town.

I'm not going to weigh myself down to no purpose. My black bag will do the trick. A pair of tights; two pairs of panties; a heavy pullover; a book, no, two – the journey is a long one; sponge bag; make-up kit? Of course, it's out of the question to arrive looking drawn! What else?

The smell was growing stronger. I was looking out for a sign of disgust on the man's face. Nothing! Yet I stank of a woman who was getting wet. Earth. Entrails. Mushrooms. Sperm. All the smells in one. How can men endure it? Because they want to fuck. It's as simple as that.

I didn't really have the choice: either I stayed outside wandering about, or I went back with him.

When the lamp in the ceiling streaked his little room with arcs of light, I noticed three postcards stapled together in a fan shape above his bed. One showed Our Lady of Fatima; the second, an American star; the last one, the Pope. I felt stupidly reassured. The man motioned that I should lie down on the nylon counterpane.

What else? So what can a young woman take with her who has decided to avenge herself, hm? That's it, a revolver! No other weapon permits a more feminine revenge: plant oneself on one's legs glistening with silk, thrust out one's pelvis to hold oneself steady, take out this mother-of-pearl knick-knack from a black handbag and point it at the man's chest, aiming at the hollow line of the ribcage.

'*You are a virgin,*' he was repeating, dumbfounded. I nodded, sitting cross-legged on the bed after he had attempted to penetrate me, in vain. I had read in a handbook on sexual education that the thickness of the hymen varied with the girl. That mine was so resistant filled me with pride; I saw in this a further proof of my moral strength. I had given no hint of any movement, waiting for him to flag. At a certain moment, I thought something was being revealed to me: this strained face which I didn't dare look at directly was life, real life; and existence, this impossible deflowering in a furnished room in Lisbon beneath some coloured postcards.

Have done once and for all with him. Shoot him down. I'm fantasizing! The writer would make a poor victim and I a second-rate murderess.

As I had guessed, I hadn't chanced upon an animal. At first, he had tried to imprison my hand around his prick, then seeing my disgust, my fatigue, he had jerked himself off on the edge of the bed, his face turned towards the wall like a child who has been punished. I didn't know what to feel: contempt, pity, tenderness for this man who masturbated alone in his room like me. The more I looked at him, the more I felt overwhelmed by a ridiculous love for others, men or women, my abandoned fellow creatures.

Presto, as soon as he had come he jumped to his feet, disappearing to return a second later with a terry towel in his hand. Like a good housewife . . . He rubbed the lino, the counterpane, everywhere where his sperm had squirted . . . Leaving no stain, no trace. When everything was cleaned up, he offered me a coffee. I thanked him, making him understand that I wanted to leave. Out of a casket decorated with seashells, he took a banknote which he handed to me for a taxi. I wedged it under my bra strap.

Some air! A cool wind whipped me in the face. I shook myself in the humid Lisbon night, my hair dishevelled, pounding the pavement, free!

Free! I repeated while tearing up his telegram. What binds me to the writer apart from my curiosity to find myself in his novel? If he didn't write, I should never have confided in him. I wonder what he is going to do with my confidences. A cloying best-seller with a sexy little girl as his heroine, modelled on the whims of an ageing man! I can imagine the title *Confessions of a Girl* standing out in pink lettering against the photo of a nymphette wearing socks. That is how he sees me. It isn't me! Why shouldn't I, myself, describe me? Why shouldn't I write this novel?

I am biting my nails. The blood runs. I suck it; it is sweet. I look for my cigarettes. There is only one left in the packet; broken.

I don't know why I'm feeling carried away. I kick my desk. The chipboard plank collapses along with biros, books, the telephone, a cup, a bottle of eraser fluid and a collection of photos. As it fell, the bottle opened and spattered them. I pick them up at once, wipe them with a handkerchief, then spread them out on my bed to let them dry.

Eighteen photos – eighteen chapters of my life. 1968–1980. Pictures replace words.

The first one: a school photo framed by a Marie-Louise in pale cardboard. June 1968. Seated at my desk in a tartan blouse, I really am cute with my bunches and my phoney look! If I had died at eight, Mummy would have affixed this photo to the porcelain vignette of my gravestone. Family tradition. All our departed have their vignettes. These touched-up portraits, with blue their dominant colour, lend an ingenuousness to them which they did not have when alive. Painted on porcelain, the members of my family become characters from a novel: my aunt who died of an adulterous love at forty, my cousin struck by lightning in the fullness of youth, my grandfather the village mayor, my adventurer uncle. My tombstone would evoke the more insignificant image of a child who died too soon.

I am photographed with my arms crossed in front of a school book. In the preceding years, the photographer would bring us together in the covered playground for a group portrait. 'The best-behaved in front!' he used to joke. I was pushed into the first row.

True, I was well behaved for a long time; so well behaved that the teacher used to summon me to her desk when she had to be away. Timid, I didn't dare call out to my friends who would get up, chatter noisily, and from their satchels take out copies of *Pif* and *Match* for the pictures of stars and corpses, and porn books.

Somebody threw me one in the course of a prolonged absence by the teacher. Nothing terribly wicked: a shadow show of ten positions. Seeing my confusion, the entire class burst out laughing: 'Oh she's so immature, oh she's so immature!'

Another photo. 1973. My friends were right: I really was a frump. At thirteen, I was still wearing high socks and a checked dress tied at the waist. Didn't I have enough self-confidence to refuse to allow Mummy always to buy me clothes at the *Lutin Bleu*? And that way of squeezing my hands together as though I were praying! In this pious little hypocrite I hardly recognize the precocious girl I thought I was, the one who used to masturbate in her bedroom, shoot up with ether, lap up her dark blood.

Yet this heavy body is my own, this podgy stomach, this moonlike face with its generous cheeks belong to me. Which is telling the truth? My memory or this photo?

With my fingers clenching the glazed paper, I scrutinize which part is truth, which lie, even the daisy threaded through the collar buttonhole of my dress – was I romantic? – even my stooped back – was I a sickly child? My mind is wandering.

In this photo, I have the moist look of a dog in front of his master. I have faith in life, a little domesticated, trusting animal. 'Father, I place my life in your hands', that is the title I would give to this photo. All is lost. My faith. My animal confidence in God's love. At thirteen I only knew that love. Boys made me blush. I had never seen a cock. I had never dared surprise my father in the bathroom. I was familiar with only one person's genitals: my own. I had never passed by the local exhibitionist, old Lafleur. My girlfriends claimed that, as they went by, he used to part the tails of his beige raincoat, show his 'thing', then do his mac up again just as a bat refolds its wings. He was fearful like a bat. I would have spared him a smile, if he had come to meet me. I wanted to love my fellow man as I did myself. My eyes dripped with love. The world was simple, like the 'good morning everyone' with which I would greet the friends of my parents, the neighbours, the tradesmen. What a nice little girl!

Seeing these eighteen negatives lined up one after another as if on a contact sheet, my laughter turns into a giggle of pain. I am seeing innocence dying; lined up in chronological order, eighteen bodies recount its death throes.

Gawky body in the first five photos. Body of a virgin. Warm look of a dog. Look which has no idea of pleasure.

1978–1979. Since I made love, the dimple of my left cheek has disappeared. In its place, my first coition has stamped a woman's grin.

1980. My first fellation taught me the art of the sidelong glance. I eye my objective slyly, seeking out the photographer's look (Pascal, my first love), provoking his desire which erects his penis when he presses the button.

Last chapter. The end of the novel. My body disintegrates.

I could have given in to anguish. I would have made for the kitchenette. I would have taken a pot of soft white cheese with 20% fat content out of the fridge. I would have stirred the smooth cheese with my finger. As I sniffed it, I would have let it drop. I would have opened a box of pure butter shortbread, then a bar of chocolate with whole hazelnuts. Burping, retching, I would have sobbed like Catherine, Mummy, like all the women of creation who cannot bear to grow up, to grow old, to fuck with soft, yielding fannies. Like them, I would have cried. Like them, I would have eaten smooth, creamy things, jellied flans. I would have given in.

I threw the photos into the sink. I applied a lighter. My cotton socks, my plump thighs began to turn brown. A small flame pierced my warm eyes. My doglike look flared up. My childhood blazed. May it rest in peace.

On a rectangular visiting card I wrote down three phrases in red capitals underlined twice.

RESOLUTION NO 1: WRITE.
RESOLUTION NO 2: WRITE FROM LIFE.
RESOLUTION NO 3: OBSERVE. TAKE NOTES. GO OUT.

I stuck the card up above my desk. From this evening onwards, I was going to take heed of it. Into a bag I slipped a biro and a spiral notebook like the writer's. My first notebook. My first sortie as an artist: I was done with giddy laughter, with languid glances, so arousing after seven o'clock. Tonight my mind would be alert.

I returned home towards midnight. The taxi dropped me in the avenue de Clichy. I had just enough to pay the fare. I got back to my studio by a narrow street which only the local inhabitants use. Its decayed hotels, immigrant bars and furnished rooms with their smashed windowpanes make it seem more disturbing than it really is.

My gait was not as assured as usual: I was moving ahead with nothing on beneath my dress: my underwear in my bag. Immediately a solitary passer-by approached, I quickened my pace, assumed a surly look, convinced he would guess that I was naked and make advances.

Nobody bothered me. I puffed with relief as I bolted the door. While some coffee was warming up again, I slipped on a kimono. I settled down in front of the typewriter. I opened my notebook. In the restaurant, I had succeeded in taking some notes without attracting the attention of the man who had asked me out.

'*La Coupole* was coming to life at night when I entered wearing pink. Hive of elegant women. The head waiter greeted me with a smile. Distinctive Parisian girl . . . '

I consult my notes: 'Central bouquet: yellow and red gladioli.

'C. waiting for me in front of a martini, his elbows on the table.

'His Jacquard pullover tight around the armholes.

'Talk through my nose. Don't have a handkerchief.'

C. was to have the signal privilege of sleeping with me at the end of three hours of chatter, two French onion soups, a coquille St Jacques with béchamel sauce and a steak with a red-wine sauce. As we waited, we prattled.

I was simpering, puckering up my lips, raising my eyebrows in the astonishment of the *ingénue*. When I laughed, my ear-rings would clink. I dipped a finger into the *entrecôte* sauce. I pulled a face, aping the capricious child. He ruffled my hair. He seemed content.

We had been talking for two hours. I rose to my feet. I wiggled my bottom on the way to the lavatory. As I went past, the waiters nudged each other, chuckling. I got my breath back on the lavatory seat. Caught in the trap of my eyelids, blue stars were twinkling.

The couples having dinner together were making me feel sick. I would gladly have spared myself this evening, had I not decided to go out more, to encounter more people. I thought that I had 'to have lived' before writing.

During dinner C. did not stop talking. The more I

listened, the more he talked.

'Women are obliged to listen to men talking. They have so many wars to tell about . . . The reverse is amusing but as "anti-glamorous" as it is possible to be.'

Psychologies, no. 84, October 1983

In the taxi we passed without any transition to the silent discourse of tongues rubbing against each other. The vehicle came to a halt; we were still kissing while the driver repeated mockingly, 'Are you getting out here?'

'A hippopotamus collection. In *cloisonné*, sandstone, papier mâché, porcelain.

'Jazz records.

'Electric aquarium.

'The lights came on as soon as we entered the room, giving out a diffused brightness. A dozen exotic fish were swimming awkwardly amid the seaweed, skirting round the miniature reproduction of a galleon and a small diver in yellow plastic.

'We were lying on a window seat – C. was kneading my breasts – when I noticed two fish swimming towards the glass wall. One of them with delicate muslin fins glued its globulous eyes against the pane of glass. It was jeering at me. It smiled at our contortions. It made fun of C.'s efforts to make me come. I no longer felt his caresses. C. took me under the watchful gaze of the fish. When he collapsed on his side, I sat up. I announced that I was going to leave. He got to his feet to call for a taxi. I stuffed my bra and panties into my bag.

'I left C. as though I had come to borrow a book off him. A white Peugeot 504 was humming outside the porch.'

Full stop! I stretch out in front of the mirror.

Dishevelled, with rings of tiredness under my eyes and a kimono gaping open at my breasts, I have the look of an artist.

I asked Hélène out to Angelina's. Proust used to go to this tea-room under the arches of the rue de Rivoli. For a week now I have been consulting writers' biographies, doing my best to discover the secret of their art in the minor details of their daily lives.

Hélène is all flesh, all smiles: side effects of love. She has finally met the man of her life. I leapt at the opportunity; my manuscript will be the richer for confessions. The writer has spoken to me very highly of their usefulness for the novel.

Hélène has ordered a *mont-blanc*, the speciality of the house. She crunches it with her beautiful teeth, not bothering to wipe her mouth powdered with meringue. The woman in love becomes a child again. After licking her fingers, Hélène announces that she really wants to eat another one, that Joel, her new love, likes her round and that she no longer has to watch her figure.

I offer her the cake which I haven't touched. She slides it on to her plate, saying that I could have enjoyed it without worrying: I have lost weight . . . She breaks off her sentence in the hope that I will talk. I pretend I haven't heard. She's right. I have started a diet. I wish to lose the last of my plumpness.

'Describe your prince charming.'

Hélène indicates that she can't talk with her mouth full. I pour her some tea. Her happiness moves me.

'He's tall, dark. One of his eyes is brown, the other green.'

'So that's why you chose him!'

'Stop making fun of me!'

'So he's good-looking. Is he good in bed?'

'You're so unromantic!'

Hélène likes me being rude to her. Hélène, the goody-goody, envies my impulses. She gets strength from my lack of concern. For her, I am 'a bad example' which she is dying to resemble.

'However, it is "the" criterion.'

'What do you call a good lover?'

'Thoughtful, imaginative. How does he kiss you?'

Hélène looks at me, flabbergasted.

'A kiss is a kiss. Joel kisses me like everybody else!'

Like everybody else! She could have tried to use her imagination. If there aren't thirty-six ways of kissing, there are countless ways of describing it. My first lover kissed like everybody else. But just as one gives a nondescript outfit the personal touch through embroidery and ribbons, so my memory has embellished our embraces.

I lapped up his palate with my tongue. I clasped his lips in mine. On some occasions I would hardly open my mouth, at others, I welcomed his breath like a gust of fresh air.

We kissed everywhere: in bars, taxis, buses; against the handrail of the stairs which ascend towards Sainte-Geneviève from the rue Monge, when he returned home to his parents after lectures. He would bend me over the boots of cars, stand me up against no-parking signs, against parking meters. He dragged me into telephone boxes. The narrower the shelter, the better the kisses.

Paris opened out its map of tenderness. We avoided the crowded, green spaces. Urban furnishings were an invitation to make a stop.

We kissed for the sake of it. We exchanged saliva like Amazonian Indians when they feed their children, by slipping a little masticated meat between their lips. We kissed for fun.

We were still kissing after we had stopped loving each other.

It took Hélène five forkfuls to polish off the almond tart.

She gives expression to her greed; a rare quality in a woman. Many conceal it as a vice, as though it were shameless to salivate, to open one's mouth wide, to shove into it a potato cooked in fat and a quarter of sole coated with *beurre blanc* sauce, to imprison the fragrant mouthful between one's tongue and palate, to crush it against one's teeth, to chew it, to swallow it feeling pleasure bursting forth and fading away.

'You, at least, don't pretend.'

Hélène throws me a suspicious glance.

'What are you insinuating?'

'You don't hide your pleasure.'

'What are you talking about? Cakes?'

'And other things. Joel, for example. Stop pulling that face! I'm only thinking of that, agreed. You don't complain. Haven't you often claimed that I liberated you from your family's puritanism. In my view, you haven't entirely shaken yourself free of it . . . '

'What are you getting at?'

'Have you slept with Joel?'

She nods.

'Did you come?'

She scrapes the rim of her plate with her fork, hesitating to reply, torn between the bashfulness of the girl in love and her desire to go on talking about him for ever. Her love. Blushing, she admits that she hasn't 'really come'.

'Is Joel aware of this?'

'No. I've pretended.'

'Just to keep him happy.'

'So he doesn't think I'm frigid! A frigid Jewish girl,

110

inconceivable! Delilah demythologized! Don't worry, I have already had orgasms. But not with Joel, doubtless because I love him too much. Sometimes I feel ashamed that I didn't know him as a virgin, that I took pleasure in the arms of other men.'

'Why don't you explain this to him?'

'He would refuse to understand. If I love him, I should come. It's as simple as that for him. Rather than get bogged down in endless explanations, I prefer to dissemble. It's child's play. You only have to cry out, pant, if needs be scratch them on the back at the right moment for them to be satisfied.'

'And reassured. Do you think that they too dissemble?'

'How can you pretend to ejaculate? With a plastic pear full of sperm!'

'I'm sure they don't come every time they ejaculate. If only they had the courage to talk about it . . . We would make love better.'

'We would finally manage to love each other. Joel really isn't talkative during those moments. I'm not asking him to overwhelm me with endearments – one shouldn't overdo it – but to talk about his pleasure. He remains speechless. Why? Does he look upon his enjoyment as a weakness?'

We fall silent, each rapt in her own thoughts. Why don't men pour out their feelings? Why do they cry out so rarely? Why do they groan when they could bellow without fear, abandon themselves in our sighs, sink into our depths? My loves are speechless as well. I sometimes have the impression that they're dead. Pleasure erases their features just as water swells the faces of drowned men, leaving each one identical to another, similar to enormous fish with their eyelids closed. The bridges of the noses fade. The arches of the eyebrows melt away. The skin tightens like a stocking on a leg.

R. resembles N. who resembles P. who resembles . . . R. is going to come. I stare at his mouth. I am waiting for a moan; silence still.

Hélène asks what is making me pensive.

'The *mont-blanc* I am going to order. This conversation has given me back my appetite. This time it's me who is going to follow your example.'

I wink at her. Hélène draws me to her by my neck and kisses me. How sweet is the complicity of women!

With its facade in a mosaic of yellow and black, its plasterwork advertisements displayed as trophies above the counter, its formica chairs and odd cups, I could hardly fail to like *Chez René*. It is the ideal place to play at being a writer. A neighbourhood bistro which adopts you very quickly if you don't put on airs.

I already have my own corner. 'Away from the door, you won't be disturbed,' the proprietress assured me pointing to a round table on the left of a tray spilling over with ferns. On it she places a small bitter cup of black coffee, hardly syrupy at all. The espresso of my freedom.

I have left university to 'devote' myself to writing, as I announced to my friends. They said that they envied, admired and supported me and would leap on my novel immediately it came out. I feel very proud.

I am less so. My novel is stagnating. In the evening I tear up the pages composed in the morning under the kindly eye of the proprietress who, of course, knows that I write.

I am becoming entangled in childhood memories, draped in categorical opinions – 'The memory is cruel. There are no women in despair' – lost in digressions which like snakes and ladders send me back to the starting square.

I await the writer's return. I need him to write as one needs an enemy to fight. Midday. I haven't strung two sentences together. The bistro is gradually filling up.

House painters, workers, a few sales reps and the students from the nearby technical college, like those two girls there who have installed themselves next to me, shouting out: 'One toasted cheese and ham, one salami and two lemonades and mint, with lots of mint!'

They attracted my attention as they came in. I immediately sized up their irregular though not unattractive faces on which their lipstick looks stained, their cheap clothes, fake Vuitton bags and coloured hair slides, which pull their hair up behind their temples. 'Future part-time secretaries,' I murmured with the satisfaction that I wasn't like them. That was what my mother used to think, faced wih her neighbours, sisters-in-law, the women of the mushroom farm who passed under her windows every morning, when she said: 'These poor people, never to have left their area.'

'Can I borrow your ashtray?'

The piercing voice of the redhead made me start.

'What do you want?'

'The ashtray.'

I hand it over, dragging out a smile for her. The blonde takes out a packet of Gauloises and a small lighter from a wallet. I observe them cutting up their toasted sandwich into tiny squares, sniggering at the arrival of a young worker, lighting cigarette after cigarette, admiring each other's rings. Superficial, chattering, teasing in their short skirts.

Wasn't I like this the first time in the Fever? Didn't I arouse in the writer the mixture of condescension and affection which they inspire in me? Little sisters whom I will never know. To whom I will never speak. From whom everything separates me: preoccupations, tastes, thoughts, ideals. Who snub me. Whom I ignore but who disturb me like a caricature of myself.

'Men are so mean! When they cough up, they want to get their money's worth. If they take you to an expensive restaurant, sure, you're going to do it.'

'Not always.'

114

The serious voice of her friend surprises me. I had associated her artificial blondness with a shrill voice.

'Only yesterday a guy came up to me in the Luxembourg . . . '

The redhead stubs out her Gauloise. I prick up my ears.

'. . . claiming he was attracted to me, that instinctively he knew everything about me: my name, my favourite singer. "What is my name?" I riposted in a flash, flattered that a guy of that sort − about forty, very suntanned, classily dressed − had noticed me. "Claudine," he replied without hesitation. Incredible, don't you think?'

The redhead nods. My heart has stopped or is it beating twice as fast?

'We went for a walk together. He was a good talker. He maintained that I was an only daughter, that I hadn't had a very happy childhood. I couldn't get over it. Do you understand why I accepted his offer of a drink? He took me to an unbelievably smart bar with the waiters dressed in white and armchairs which were so deep that just as we were about to leave I had difficulty standing up.'

I'm dreaming! I'm hearing voices. This girl is making it up! If I weren't to control myself, I would fling myself at her screaming: 'You lying bitch!'

The redhead asks whether he tried to kiss her. I don't know why she reminds me of Hélène; no doubt because of the cajoling intonation she adopts to question her friend.

'Not at all! He wasn't a womanizer. He hardly said a word. He listened. I must have fascinated him. "You amaze me," he kept repeating. Yet I wasn't telling him anything extraordinary. Just my life! My studies which bored me, my mother who had opposed my going into opera. He concluded that she was jealous. He scribbled down two or three words on the paper mat placed under our glasses and put it in his pocket.'

115

It's him! It's the writer! It's my writer! He has returned home from Lisbon.

After the surprise, the humiliation. That he approached this insipid blonde is what upsets me the most. So he has established connections between her and me. It is claimed that each man is only attracted to one type of woman. Do I have that dull look, that silly air? For this girl to be a caricature of me is bad enough, but for her to resemble me physically!

In the mirror which covers the wall facing me, I find I am ugly. Ugly as a woman betrayed. To do that to myself!

I regained my calm during the short distance separating the bistro from my studio. The writer was free to do what he wanted. He had replaced me. He had finally understood that I was no longer his heroine.

I went round to the rue du Temple with the draft of my novel under my arm, satisfied. The day before, I got the proprietress of *Chez René* to read it. Although she had found certain passages 'daring', she complimented me; she had read it in 'a single sitting'. Her opinion had given me confidence again, my propensity to get carried away at the slightest little thing did the rest; I had found my way! The writer had played a large part in this. I forgot the acrimony of our past encounters. I forgot everything. The heroine had given way to a budding novelist. I arrived full of hope.

When he opened the door, I thought I had got the wrong floor. I remembered sharp features, a thin nose, a beard like a tangle of Algiers yarn; I met with a beardless face. Round, heavy, hardly separated from the neck, it seemed to have been fashioned by an impatient hand, which in its haste had forgotten about the chin and botched up the ears. I felt I had been duped. I recalled one Christmas I discovered a dolly, when I had believed in the promise of a bicycle. My enthusiasm waned.

The writer announced that he had shaved his beard off the day before: 'As I was writing my novel, my desire to progress barefaced grew.'

'Why did you grow a beard?'

'I can admit it now: for aesthetic reasons. I have a weak chin, a wide jawbone . . . "A slightly prognathous

117

face", in the words of Mauriac. My beard balanced it. Oh I don't regret a thing! I have found the cheeks I had as a young man again. I am breathing more freely. Without my beard, I feel that my face is coming to life.'

I contemplate him without saying a word. He is barechested, in Levi's. His jeans, too unused, cling to his thighs. They are fleshy like a woman's.

What a mess the room is in! Magazines are strewn over the floor. On his desk a plate, containing the remains of a meal, is lying about. The sofa is littered with dirty clothes.

'You caught me right in the middle of working.'

He picks up a cushion, dusts it down and places it on a box which he pushes towards me.

I sit down heavily. How could he have changed in so short a time? He barely stayed a week in Lisbon. Is this the man whose dashing figure I have been pursuing? Is this the man who used to make me stammer on the end of a telephone? Is this him, my writer?

He has settled down on the sofa, facing me.

'I had given up hope of seeing you again after what happened.'

I gestured to make him understand that it was forgotten.

'In Lisbon, shut up in my room, I didn't stop thinking of you. It was raining. The drizzle made the Alfama look ugly. A friend had spoken to me of a bombed-out church, never rebuilt, which he compared to a ghost ship with pious old women for its crew. This was the one and only time I went out. I slipped on the wet porchway. I didn't leave my hotel again. I was plagued by remorse. How could I have been so crude towards you. I couldn't understand it. Why aren't you saying anything?'

'Don't go on. That episode is over. I haven't come to ask you to apologize but to give me hints about writing. I've started a novel.'

He pretends not to hear, casts his eyes around the room as though he were searching for something to show me. He suddenly suggests champagne.

'No thanks. I don't want to drink but work. You ought to be flattered that I have come to you.'

'It's a real pleasure! I am the only writer you have met!'

'How do you know? I'm charming! Evidently! I'm interesting to talk to! I could have gone to the Fever while you were away and subdued one of your chums! And when I say "chums" . . . '

'What are you talking about?'

I leap to my feet.

'Nervy little thing, aren't we!'

'Listen, I have hardly any time to spare. Either I show you what I have written and you can give me your opinion; or I leave and I won't ever come back, either here or to the Fever.'

He raises his eyes to the ceiling.

'Carry on! Your aggressiveness is delightful! It sends me into raptures! Your eyebrows arched in anger . . . Your quivering nostrils . . . What a woman! It makes a change from the sighs of my woman readers. If only you knew the letters they send me! Erotic adventures on blue paper or typewritten insults with names, addresses and photos. I only keep the first ones. I'll make a best-seller out of them.'

'Stop waffling on.'

I hand him the bundle of paper. He glances through it rapidly. I bite my lip. I am dreading his judgement. A slight, mocking pout plays about his mouth.

'Amusing.'

'There must be more . . . '

'Go over your dialogue again. Good dialogue can gain time. I'm working on that at the moment. You know how to observe. Your psychology on the other hand . . . '

'What do you mean by "psychology"?'

'The causes of the conscious, as of course of the unconscious mind, my dear. Why does the man in the Jacquard pullover – a somewhat scant description, wouldn't you say? – want to fuck you? Pardon this expression, I try to be of my time. You're not saying anything. This character makes me think of a Pavlovian dog: he is introduced to a pretty girl, so off he goes salivating.'

'You're being unfair . . . '

I was secretly hoping that his enthusiasm would respond to mine. That has no importance any more. He no longer interests me.

He hands me back the bundle and makes for his desk. He returns with a box of white wood.

'Here is my personal micro-encyclopaedia. Astronomy, fine arts, political theory, proverbs and prejudices, zootechny. Everything is recorded on cards measuring eleven by eighteen centimetres. Pick one out at random. What do you read?'

' "All criticism starts first of all with a criticism of religion." Who is that by?'

He snatches the card from my hands.

'By Marx,' he mutters. 'An old note. I should have thrown it out. What do you think of this?

It is evening, autumn
I think solely
Of my parents

A haiku of the best vintage. I dream of writing a novel in haikus!'

He can go to hell with his psychology, his cards and haikus! I wanted specific advice, the tricks of the trade, something concrete! If he is reluctant to give me some, it is because he considers me to be a rival. So when he covers his manuscript with his hand like that, he is afraid that I will put him in the shade! What a coward! I have nothing left to do here!

He hasn't noticed my restlessness and is still rummaging about in his box.

'And this one:

> *Full moon*
> *And on her plaits*
> *The shadow of a pine*

Sublime, don't you think?'

'No! Dreadful! Like you! You make me sick! My
starting to write bothers you, doesn't it? You really
didn't expect it. What can a girl with a turned-up nose
say? Be quiet and let me add one or two things before I
leave. You are refusing to help me out of jealousy.'

'Ridiculous! And this box, I don't show it to
anybody!'

'What do you want me to do with your notes; most
date from 1968! Final remark: OK I've pinched your
subject. But this subject happens to be me. So watch
out!'

He sighs, his arms folded over his chest.

'What's the point? You haven't understood a thing
but let's stop this discussion, it won't get us anywhere.
We won't escape the fate of the sexes! You are a
woman, I had forgotten. In giving you my trust, I acted
as a man. Our weakness is to believe in your integrity,
ladies. Not that women are dishonest; they are calcu-
lating. Their instinct quickly yields to tactical con-
siderations. I ought to have remembered this ever
since we first met.'

I make a show of standing up. He seizes me by my
sleeves.

'Before you leave, can I ask you one last favour?'

I ask him what, while twiddling a strand of hair
around my nose.

'That of seeing you again.'

Thinking prevents writing. If I had brought the typewriter to the rue du Temple, I would have placed it on the pavement immediately after I had left the flat and I would have hit the keys, humming in the excitement of my victory. 'The writer wants to see me again. The ball is in my court.' The joyful tapping would have come to a halt only at dusk. I would have been overcome by the cold. I would have arrived back at the studio, the leaves of paper in my hand. I would have continued to write until dawn.

Wonderful dreams. Nothing is coming. Words, sentences are drifting: 'Fate, haiku, hints, dialogue; you know how to observe. Your aggressiveness is delightful.' The smell of lavender persists on his skin. When he sat down on the sofa, the leatherette's smooth surface appeared even greyer.

Leatherette, chest, seat . . . car . . . The word particles are drawn to each other; a memory arranges itself. Another body is superimposed on the writer's, younger, clad in cotton trousers and a light sweatshirt. Planted on the leatherette seat of a 4L, a man is driving, one hand on the wheel, the other on my knee. A black beard darkens his face. In profile he looks like a visionary by El Greco. Tense mouth, fixed look of brother Felix Hortentio Paravicino whose coloured reproductions decorated a history book. We came across each other in a provincial museum an hour ago. We were the only visitors. We had understood.

In the hotel I murmured that he should wait for me by room twenty-six. In his haste he left the door ajar. He collapsed on the bed. He stretched out and without a sigh pitched on to me, concentrating hard as in the 4L. He weighed a lot. His ribcage crushed me. I was suffocating under the mass of muscles and flat ribs like logs. When he penetrated me, his chest impaled me. He came soundlessly, then rolled on to his side. His chest jutted out even more. Chrysalis ready to open out, brown shell bursting with life. A moment ago, his heart was beating like a moth caught in the white-hot trap of a lamp. His swarthy chest frightened me. I thought back to the primitive Christ put up behind the altar of a Catalan church. I went to see it every summer: its broad hands, rugged bust, thrown-out ribcage terrified me. This wasn't Our Lord but a mountain man crucified in the flower of his life, a man like no other I had seen before. Every summer I expected him to come down from the cross and crush me against his chest of oak. I announced to the young man that I didn't want to see him again.

I like straightforward, heedless, inconsequential love; fleeting embraces, bodies which topple over. I can do without proof; sweat is enough. Odour of passion. He sweats therefore he loves me. When bodies are dry, people leave each other. I hate croissants when I wake up, and promises.

Yet I have known Pierre for six months now. We see each other three times a week. We must have had seventy breakfasts together. We have had intimate dinners a hundred or so times; a hundred or so times we have made love.

Habits replace feelings.

I sleep on the left against the wall. He brings me an orange juice in the morning. We listen to Bach, drinking our coffee. I have a wash while he tidies up the kitchen. I do the dishes; he performs his *toilette*. The mechanism works. Sometimes he jars and trust, sexual pleasure, the moral code, feminist precepts – wheels within wheels – seize up. An argument, a kiss and everything restarts. Putting the parts together is sufficient for there once again to be daylight in the bedroom, for him to wake me up by kissing the tip of my nose, for me to go to the loo before he gets up, etc.

He is a patient lover. He is living an adventure. Since he was twenty (he knew womankind two days after his twentieth birthday), he has conceived of sexuality as a journey of initiation. This isn't his idea. That he cribbed it from a book doesn't alter anything. If certain men lose their good manners in bed, he remains a boy scout. He wants to do things properly. He is afraid of displeasing me. When he asks me whether I like 'doing that', I perceive a slight anxiety in his voice.

He demonstrates initiative; I, goodwill. A single act disgusts me: swallowing sperm. Fellation reminds me of poses: my mouth reaching out for the Host, my tongue ready to fasten on to it. I spit it out. He observes me. He doesn't dare say a thing. He is wondering whether the sperm wouldn't make her feel sick if it wasn't his. Would he swallow his own sperm if he were a woman? He smiles at me. I don't think he minds. I would like to make the effort. Impossible, my entire body stiffens in refusal.

Because of one summer's evening in London?

I had been sent there to brush up my English. I was taking the *baccalauréat* that year. The family putting me up had a son, Andrew. Twenty-two years old. He was a barman in a pub in North Finchley. That evening he came home earlier. A fight had broken out between hooligans. The police closed the pub. I heard him coming up the stairs. His room was next to mine. He entered. I gave a start; I was reading in bed wearing blue pyjamas. He came towards me. His eyes shone like buttons on ankle boots.

'You're drunk.'

124

He told me to lower my eyes. He had his penis out in the air. I didn't move, just like the mongoose who waits fascinated for the cobra, desires it, provokes it by remaining motionless, knowing in advance that the combat is lost. He seized my hand and squeezed it around his rod. His penis swelled; the vein on his forehead swelled as well. He hurt me crushing my neck so that I lowered my head to the height of his cock.

'Look, that's sperm.'

It was going to spurt . . . No, only a drop, then a colourless jelly. He let go of my neck, wiped his forehead and went out, closing the door with care so as not to awaken his 'folks'. I went to find a flannel. I wiped off the sperm. Childhood was growing fainter.

So that's what it was. That sort of white glue. So why those blushes, allusions, half-smiles; why that periphrasis or those words: 'seed, semen, sperm, spunk, juice'?

The phone rings. Pierre's clear voice. Adorable Pierre. He spruces himself up before my visits. Hair cream, after-shave, a shirt which matches his eyes. I kiss him on the neck. I sniff him, rubbing my nose over his chest just like a bitch recognizing her puppy. I finger his fleshy shoulder. I pass a hand under his shirt to check the softness of his stomach. He is proud of this body which he knows is silky and muscled. He has given himself the nickname of 'the stallion'.

We will spend the weekend together in Fontainebleau.

Pierre's house in the country is the last one in the village. You can scent the forest from the terrace.

It doesn't stop raining. We walk all over the deserted village eagerly. Our feet are lost in these rubber boots found in the cellar. Mine are taking in water. I don't care, overjoyed to splash about in the puddles. Bodily euphoria. I'm young. I realize this suddenly. The most trifling thing is enough: running for no reason; a desire to sing at the top of my voice, to tear off a syringa branch which protrudes over a gate, to kick a pebble as though it were life that you sent flying into the air.

We follow the road which leads to the forest. Cars hoot at us, splash us. We laugh.

Pierre suggests that we take path number eighty-six as far as the Apremont gorges. The wet sand weighs down our steps. We have been walking for three hours. I trip on a pine root which has forced back the rock in order to grow. We will go onwards until we are exhausted.

I am worn out! I slump on to the sofa. Pierre springs towards the fireplace without even taking off his K-Way. He really is adorable! I stretch myself out. Fatigue pours into my body like molten bronze.

Of course we are going to make love! In front of the flames the colour of alcohol, the colour of the grog which we are drinking, snuggled up against each other. Country silence, smell of rum and warm bodies, sofa covered with an animal skin, crackling of flames: the setting is fixed. We won't escape it.

One book marked my adolescence, *Jacquou the Bumpkin*, I kept it by my bedside. Before I fell asleep, I would always read the same passage when the daughter of Count Nansac, caught by the shower, finds refuge in the dilapidated cottage of the serf.

Jacquou is stoking up the fire. Chemisettes and a petticoat are drying on the end of the bench installed in the hearth. Smell of grass and soaking bodies. Same smells. Same colours. Ochres, browns, ambers. Colours of the grog, leaves, pubs for lager. Sienna earth, honey, coffee-brown, colours of superfine tights which the woman slips over her legs under the gaze of the man sprawled on the sofa.

Everything becomes blurred. My reading, my walks, the Sunday-evening film, the pubs and the flames.

'Pierre, have you seen *Love*, the film by Ken Russell? Do you remember the scene in which Birkin and Gerald are struggling naked in front of a colossal fireplace?'

Women in Love. Yet another book from my adolescence. I discovered *Lady Chatterley's Lover* a little later. Shut up in my bedroom, I used to read it in translation with the English text next to it, passing from one version to the other.

His hands on her loins. *Ses mains sur ses reins.* Her bottom: *son cul à elle.* His root: *sa bite.* She caresses his root. He covers her with flowers. In the heart of the woods. It rains.

I have taken off my clothes. I undress Pierre, striking a pose between each button. He lets himself go. His skin retains the sweet-smelling dampness of the forest. I put my hand out . . . he sits up on his forearms and suggests that we go up to the room.

'Don't you feel good here?'

'No, up there we'll have more peace and quiet.'

'Are you afraid of voyeurs?'

Pierre pulls his jeans up again and without a word takes me up to the first floor.

The room is furnished 'rustic Breton' style. To the right of the door and covered in red braided cretonne, a bed with village scenes carved in the frame; opposite, a wardrobe with three doors in the same manner; to its left, a rectangular mirror fastened to the wall by chrome hooks. Double curtains to match the counterpane. I fall to my knees on the carpet.

Pierre is getting an erection in front of the mirror. He admires himself, his groin thrust out towards my mouth, his legs parted. How handsome he is, my little colossus! His cock stands out against the fleur-de-lis wallpaper like a collage. He directs it towards my lips. I suck it like a straw.

'Look how hard I am for you!'

Grabbing hold of me by my hair, he forces me to turn my head towards the mirror. I resist, my throat bursting with his flesh. I don't want to look. Absolutely not! I wish he would shoot his load quickly! Take it out! Leave me alone! I am sucking non-stop. Nausea is rising.

He is swaying, his eyes half-closed, his neck sagging backwards, far from me. I hazard a brief look, just the time to notice a bent body and breasts which are juddering. My flesh seems flaccid next to Pierre's, in the brace of pleasure. My breasts hang like udders. I have my mother's heavy breasts. I go on looking; I have my mother's submissive body.

Pierre is still rocking a vast way off from me. If he wasn't going to come at any moment, I would have released his cock; I would have laughed, sobbed. With that cock in my mouth swelling my cheeks, my face looks like a *commedia dell'arte* mask. Pantaloon . . .

By his ever more rapid toings and froings I sense that Pierre . . . I still keep it between my lips . . . I open my mouth in time.

We returned home the next day, the boot brimming with heather. He dropped me off at Porte de Vanves station.

I go down to La Fourche. My rapid step chases away the pigeons of the avenue de Clichy. They flutter about, place themselves a few metres further off and begin to peck at the asphalt again. Some Arabs are shouting at each other as they unload crates of Webb lettuces. I can hear the south. The freshness of the night lingers in the plane trees; in an hour, the gas from the exhaust pipes will have absorbed it like blotting paper.

Walking past the porchway, I greet the concierge standing in front of her lodge. As she always has the air of waiting for something or someone, I have nicknamed her 'Madame Godot'.

'You know, when you go off, you should perhaps warn your admirers!'

I turn round towards the short figure who is advancing with her hands shoved into the central pocket of her apron.

In a sing-song voice, I ask her whether I have had visitors. My concierge eyes me up and down severely.

'Yesterday, at eleven o'clock at night. A madman was crying out hoarsely in the courtyard: "Elisa, Elisa!" I had to get up.'

'I'm sorry . . . '

'I don't mind, I don't sleep at night. But even so, it's not a decent time to pay a call.'

There is the hint of a faint smile on her face, overjoyed to keep me in suspense. The one time I have listened to her.

'What was he like, your gentleman?'

'I didn't like the look of him, I really hesitated before replying. He wanted to know which floor you lived on. As I have never seen you with him, I was on my guard.'

'You didn't ask him his name?'

'I would not have taken the liberty! I am not indiscreet. If you want a piece of advice, watch out for him, he isn't on the level. Unshaven, an odd look. You might think he took drugs. He doesn't have an honest-looking face, that one! As I refused to show him your flat, he took out a crumpled scrap of paper saying: "Is this enough to let me in?" Your name and phone number. I recognized your writing . . . '

'Did you tell him where I lived?'

She shrivels up like a grandmother who is refused a sweet.

'I had to. I was afraid. I read in *Le Parisien* that sadists are laying into old people . . . '

I take her by the shoulder.

'You did the right thing. Don't worry, that man won't be coming back again. Here, so I'm forgiven.'

I hand her my bouquet of heather. She grasps it without thanking me: 'It's beautiful but I wonder whether I have a big enough vase.'

On the landing I notice an envelope wedged in the embrasure of the door.

Elisa,

I have searched so hard for you that I have almost gone blind. Not knowing either your name or your address, I combed through the phone numbers of two directories. My eyes are burning but I do finally know where you live. Elisa, I have to see you at the earliest opportunity. Ever since your visit, I have no longer managed to write. I have abandoned my novel. My hand is as though dead. I think only of you. We can't be without each other. I need you to draw me from this impotence; you need me, to write. You have talent. I undertake to find you a publisher. But for pity's sake, answer me!

Naturally the letter isn't signed. I fold it nervously back into the envelope. The playacting is over. I have had enough of a sick man trying it on. My concierge was right. He is mad. Writer? Forgotten writer! A literary prize in the sixties, some interviews, some highly favourable reviews, a few television programmes; then oblivion; indifference. Silence for no reason. He never recovered from it. Since then he has hung around in bars, the notebook which is his alibi in his pocket, as pitiable as an old tragedienne bloated by gin and memories. I'm being unfair. He cut a fine figure when I met him. He really looked a writer. Author of *romans-à-clef*. Caustic. Brilliant. The silk neckerchief. The sonorous laugh. The supple legs. The effortless ability. Suddenly the transformation. Impotence. He himself employed this word.

I open up the letter to check. I hadn't noticed the blue colour of the paper. A reflection returns to me: 'If only you knew the pleasure I take in reading about their erotic adventures on blue paper.' Was he calling his female admirers to mind or . . . what if it were a . . . Absurd! I'm not going to begin fantasizing as well. *Basta*!

My lipstick clashes with my outfit. I have taken too long to change. The door slams. I tear down the stairs while at the same time sticking one final pin into my chignon. I have put my dress on inside out! I stop. The stair light goes out. In the darkness I pop out of the sheathe of jersey by wriggling my hips. It is so tight, this dress! My panties must be showing through.

Hélène is giving a fancy-dress party. I am going as a prostitute. I've dreamt of doing this for ages! Here I am kitted up like the real thing. Blood-red mouth, doll-like eyelashes, accentuated breasts, fishnet stockings held up by a suspender belt with marguerites sown on it and flat shoes in red and black kid leather. Stiletto heels sink between the paving stones of the yard. I twirl my fake crocodile bag around like in the films. I go up the street with my rump swaying. Nobody. The tradesmen have drawn their metal shutters. I can hear steps . . .

A hand seizes my arm. A man's hand. A face emerges from the shadows. His face. The writer. He was lurking behind the container for used glass. He was on the look-out for me. Hunter spying on the teal. He was lying in wait. His hand sinks into my flesh.

'Let go of me! You're hurting!'

'Elisa, what are you doing in this get-up?'

'You've got eyes, haven't you. Leave me alone! I don't want to see you any more! Fuck off!'

I swing my bag in his face. He ducks, catches hold of

it by the shoulder strap. He pulls me towards him. I resist. He pulls harder, dragging me in front of an estate agent's. He halts against the illuminated shop window, the only one in the street.

'It really is you,' he whispers.

It really is him. Trembling lips, grimy skin and pullover. Opposite his shifty mug, my whore's face. What a shock, my face. He won't get over it. Elisa wearing little pink socks, in a suit from thingummybobs. Charming Elisa. Little Elisa: a prostitute.

He looks so lost that I could lead him by the hand as far as a taxi, entrusting him to the driver like my granny. For a little while I feel sorry for him. His loose clothes, grey skin, Adam's apple which is going up and down, his hunted look. He is perspiring. I can smell the sour odour of his skin, his breath.

'But in that case, if you're a whore . . . '

He stammers. His is the ashen voice of delirium. He has been drinking. Not a refined, Technicolor drink with a slice of pineapple and an umbrella stuck in it to look pretty. He has downed the most acidic gut-rot and he is off to screw a whore. I'm panicking. Why is this street deserted? On Saturday evening! How many charitable souls would show up if I called for help? I look up. A figure appears at a window. 'Hey, help!' The window is shut brutally. The writer turns round. I shove him away and take to my heels.

I run like hell, faster than the school champion. My shoes are making me trip. I fling them into the gutter. I would definitely take off my dress to tear along faster. Impossible to lengthen my strides. But why is this road so long? I turn round. The writer is following me. He's still far away. He looks as if he's struggling.

Running on the tarmac in fishnets really hurts. I won't be able to keep it up for long. Hold out just a few metres further. I'll take one of the three bridges which span the railway line. I'll go back up the boulevard des Batignolles. In place Clichy, I'll vanish into a brasserie.

I can't go on.

The road comes to an end in a gust of fresh air.

With my legs shaking I dash on to the bridge, seizing the guardrail straight away. I detest bridges. I cross them with my eyes shut. I can't look at the drop; it's so beautiful, the drop.

The railway line glides like a torrent at the bottom of a valley. You might think that you were in the mountains; here, no rock but rubble stones blackened by pollution. Altitude is horizontal: 'Paris-Saint-Lazare – 200m'. An orange train moves slowly away. What if I jumped? On to the train like a cowboy! Calamity Jane. Fishnets over the guardrail. Icarus. My body a kite in a floating dress. Moment of poetry. The angel's leap.

He has caught up with me. I have lingered too long on the bridge. My feet were too painful, I was too hot, too afraid. I am afraid. Fear contorts my lips into a silent cry. The blood-red crack seems to smile. I have my fish-face on, my pale, flat face of real terror.

I barely offer any resistance when he takes me round my waist, bending my arm behind my back so as to pin me against the fencing. He is trembling as much as I am.

'You can't run from me any more . . . I won't let you go before I have you, have you . . . '

He rubs up against me. My back arches over the guardrail. With my free hand I attempt to push him back; he twists my wrist.

'I have wanted you . . . ever since the first day . . . ever since the Luxembourg. I didn't dare. Your face . . . Your round cheeks . . . You could have been my daughter but you're a . . . you're a . . . a whore!'

Doll in jersey, why am I all feeble in his hands? Why am I dumb? I could explain that I have got dressed up. I might calm him, reassure him that I am fond of him at the bottom, right at the bottom of my heart, neither a woman's nor a girl's but my heart for God's sake! Lie.

Say anything at all so he doesn't touch my breast, so he doesn't squeeze it, bruise it.

'I wanted to touch you for ages . . . '

He tries to open my dress. If I don't do something, it's rape on the rue de Rome, one hundred metres above the railway line!

'Don't worry about me! Just fuck me on the bridge! I can see the headlines now: "The rapist was a writer! " '

He lets go of me, dazed, then he begins to laugh, really laugh . . .

'She fell for it as well! They all fall for it, every one of them! Me, a writer!'

He guffaws with laughter, his hand pointing at himself. His laughter grows in the whistling of a train which is entering the station. A metallic laugh. Enough!

I pushed him hard, very hard.

I ran towards the boulevard des Batignolles. Faster, yet faster; my fishnets were falling down. Men turned round as I went past; some were chortling. Me, I ran. Blood in my mouth. The boulevard seemed endless. I marked time in front of an animated scene. I reached the place Clichy in a dazzle of white headlamps and neon lighting. The smell of petrol was suffocating me. My eyes were burning. I could hardly make out the winking signs of the bars around the statue of Marshal Moncey. *Le Chalet. La Havane. Le Champagne. La Taverne du Régent.* I crossed the tiled threshold of *Le Petit Poucet* on the corner of a gloomy road. I asked a waiter for the lavatory; he pointed to the far end of the room over his tray. I walked along the bar. By the yellow light of the tulip-shaped lamps of aluminium, the customers looked like zombies. Their every glance followed me; I saw their faces in the mirror on the wall.

A spiral staircase led to the lavatory. Sawdust sprinkled the steps. The door marked 'Women' was shut; I pushed open the men's. As the bolt clicked in, the wall lamp came on.

I stripped. I masturbated standing upright, sobbing, with the sounds in my throat of an animal which is being finished off. I summoned the orgasm. The release. My temples were ringing, ringing. My heart was bursting. My fanny was rumbling. My heart . . .

A trickle of blue ran underneath the door. I had dragged down the bottle of bleach in my fall.